VULCAN

SEQUEL TO SHADOW

Printed in Australia
First printing: June 2024

Paperback ISBN 978-1-7637569-6-0
Hardcover ISBN 978-1-7637569-8-4
Ebook ISBN 978-1-7637569-7-7

Cyber Unicorns
www.cyberunicorns.com.au

A catalogue record for this book is available from the National Library of Australia

VULCAN

SEQUEL TO SHADOW

CRAIG FORD

ALSO BY CRAIG FORD

THE FORESIGHT SERIES

Foresight
Shadow
Vulcan

The Shadow World

CHAPTER 1

BACK TO REALITY

Standing, looking at myself in the mirror, I almost don't recognise myself. I am no longer a teenage girl, I am a woman. So much has happened over the last few months, I barely even remember the carefree life I had at school. I'd had no concerns, no real problems, just thinking up what my next target was going to be, who Foresight would hunt next. I didn't have to worry about work or boys, just John and myself. A simple existence; one that I miss, if I'm honest. I don't know if it's the job, the snatch and grab ordeal, or just life in general, that has made me jump from that carefree teenager to a stressed-out adult. I'm not sure my life is what my teenage self would've wanted.

It's been a few days since Shadow was arrested. I haven't been able to stop thinking about the image of him being escorted away in handcuffs. He saved my life, and together we took down some very bad people. That dark hole they've put him in isn't right. He shouldn't be there. I know he hasn't had a perfect, crime-free existence, but neither have I. We aren't much different. I could've gone down that same path if the General hadn't recruited me first. Shadow's circumstances played a big part in his journey and I don't blame him for how he reacted; I would have probably done the same thing.

He was too young to have lost his parents the way he did, to experience what he did. I can only imagine the mess of his father shooting himself in the head. That is nothing a young boy needs to see, let alone again when his mother decides the pain of her loss is too unbearable. I don't blame Shadow for being angry at the man who caused it all.

He tried to get help, get justice for his parents the right way, at least initially, until he'd realised he would have to take matters into his own hands, claim his pound of flesh from the perpetrator. He should have stopped once he got what was owed to him, but he'd filled the hole from the loss of his parents, used that pain to continue some sort of vigilante cause. It doesn't feel unreasonable to me. I'd hunted bad guys for years, inflicting my own punishment on them just like Shadow. The only difference was I didn't take their money or if I did, I didn't keep any of it.

That's the difference between us: he kept some of the money to fund his mission, I didn't. I don't think that is a reason to keep him in some horrible secret federal prison I can't even find. I have no idea where he is or how long he'll be there. But there isn't much I can do about it.

I'm heading back into the office today after a couple of days leave. I'd needed to clear my head and just breathe. To centre myself, refocus of sorts. It didn't work. I don't feel focused or ready to get back to work. It's too early to give up and just let go, to forget Shadow and move on. At some point, I might have to, but not yet. I'm not ready for that.

I walk downstairs and have some breakfast. Nothing exciting, just some toast and a coffee. John has already left for work so it's just me and my thoughts this morning. Great, just what I need. I need to follow Shadow's example on this and find a distraction. Something to take my mind off of him. Though maybe not something as suicidal as taking on a terrorist-linked hacking group. I need to get back to work and just lose myself in the next job. I'll fight for Shadow if the opportunity comes up but I need to get used to the fact that his fate is not in my hands, I can't influence that at the moment. So I will focus on what I can do, well, at least try to anyway.

I pack up my things, put the dishes in the sink, and head out the door. As I do, the sun's reflection flashes across my face from my replacement mustang; it's a dark horse, one of only a few in the country, a slight upgrade from the old one. It has armour plating and quite a bit of a power train upgrade. This thing is a little scary, if I'm honest. It feels like a screaming beast balancing on a knife's edge, teetering on losing control. I love it. At least I'll be able to have some fun on the way to the office. Nothing better than a bit of an adrenaline rush to get the brain clear. Get moving for the day, just what the doctor ordered.

The trip to work is quick. I hope I don't get any tickets. I cut it close on a few lights, moving through in a blur as the lights turned orange. I should learn to keep the pace down a little before I get the car impounded; I don't think the General would be too happy about that. I park the car at a parking facility a few streets away from work and call in a ride to shuttle me to the office. I can't take this thing anywhere near the office, it's definitely not inconspicuous, not something that would blend in at all.

The rest of the day goes by pretty fast. I'm a bit of a celebrity in the office, Shadow and I achieved pretty epic things in just a few weeks. Targets had been on the hit list for years and we'd just taken them out like it was nothing. I have to admit, what we managed to do is a big deal, but I don't think it is worth all the attention I'm getting. I just want to get on with my job and stop having to think about Shadow.

The next few days go by similarly. I go to work, do the bare minimum, then head back home to sleep. Rinse and repeat, that's all I can do. Keep moving forward and hope that I can get back to some kind of normal. It doesn't feel right at the moment. The whole world seems off-balance. It's hard to explain but it just feels wrong. I need to give myself some time though. Time is what I need.

Oh, who the hell am I kidding? Time is not what I need. I need to get Shadow out of that place. I owe him that at least. If nothing else he should be able to go free. Even if he'll be watched for the rest of his life – or at least until he loses his tail again – but some sort of freedom. He's earned that.

CHAPTER 2

THE OFFER FROM ABOVE

I'm making my way down to the General's office, I think I may be about to get the talk. You know: *I feel your work has started to slip; you don't seem to be focusing. What's wrong? We need to get past this. You need to move on. Shadow is going to be in there a long time.* That conversation. It's been coming and I know it but I really don't want to sit there and listen to it. I just want to be left to my own devices, just let me deal with it in my way. I'll get it together; I don't need an intervention by the General.

The elevator stops and the doors open to the General's lobby. I step out, allowing the security systems to do their thing and authorise my access. I walk up to the entrance, take a deep breath and enter. As I walk through into his office, the General stands up, walking around his desk towards me.

'Sam, good, thank you for coming down. I want to talk to you about something, a bit of a problem I have and maybe a solution that you might be able to help me with.' He gestures for me to sit on one of the couches in his office, big, leather monstrosities, the type you would think of in an old-school easy bar or gentlemen's club. They are quite comfortable and that concerns me.

I haven't been sleeping too well and I don't think it will go down well if I take a nap while we are meant to be talking. I need to focus, ensure I don't relax too much. He walks over to the bar. 'Can I get you a beer?' He grabs two out of the fridge before I really get a chance to answer, handing me one as he sits on the other end of the couch.

'Thanks.'

He opens his beer and I do the same. We both take a mouthful before he continues. 'Now, I've noticed that my star hacker is struggling a little and I think this is partly my fault.'

Okay, so it is going to be a pep talk, an attempt to cheer me up and get me back on the horse, so to speak. Well, I guess it was only a matter of time. I know that I haven't been very focused and I know my work is very subpar compared to my usual standards but that is still pretty good work. 'I know you don't agree with how I handled things with Shadow. He saved your life and helped bring down two very bad groups.' He pauses to take a mouthful of his beer.

I lift my bottle, doing the same, and feel the cold liquid run down my throat. It's perfect beer temperature. 'I couldn't very well let a criminal just walk free, you know that.' I go to say something, but he lifts his hand to stop me. 'There is also the issue of how well you two did. I have praise pouring down from above. They feel you should get a further promotion. They'll be expecting big things moving forward, more of these types of takedowns, more big busts, but how are we going to be able to achieve that when my best hacker is barely functioning at a quarter of her ability? You've been moping around like you haven't slept in weeks...' He fixes me with a steely look. 'What do I do about all of this, Sam?'

I shift in my seat a little. It's about to get real uncomfortable. I hate talking about myself, especially about my feelings. Is he going to ask me about how I feel about Shadow? If there is something more there, beyond just two hackers doing their jobs?

'Don't worry, I am not here to talk about your feelings or anything like that. We have shrinks if that is something you want. Is that something you want?' the General asks. I shake my head and he continues. 'I want to offer you a promotion.' He sits calmly, watching me as he lightly drums his fingers against the armrest of his chair. I don't say anything, I just hold his gaze. After a few moments he continues. 'I think it might be a solution for what we all need. A way to achieve the goals for the powers that be and allow you the ability to do it without restriction,' he says.

Okay, now I'm listening. 'What is this promotion exactly?'

He smiles and takes another mouthful of his beer. 'I've been thinking about this for a couple of days. The money that Shadow and yourself collected from Arachnid is quite a large sum and could easily fund a program for many years. This program could run completely off books. No red tape, no bureaucracy, no interference. You and your team could do what is needed, whenever it is needed. You could do it in the shadows, in complete secrecy. There would be no links to the Australian government or any of its allies. A perfect weapon against the thugs of this world and we could have complete ability to deny any involvement.'

A black ops hacker squad, in essence, that's what he is talking about. 'So, you want me to run this hacker squad of sorts? To run off-book jobs as we did with Arachnid, essentially hunt down the worst of the worst and then find a way to take them down? Take their money, take their assets and do it with complete autonomy? Have I got that right?'

He just nods slowly and gives me a single syllable response. 'Yes'.

That could be a worthwhile job. I could make a difference, a real difference, every day.

'What's the catch?' I ask. There's always a catch.

He nods slowly. 'Yes, there is a catch. The fact is that because this is a black ops team, you will not have the protection of the ASD. You'll be on your own. If you get caught, we will not be able to help you, at least in the short term. You'll have to rely on yourself and your team. You would be out in the cold, needing to fend for yourself.'

That was what I would expect, and the condition doesn't cause real concern, if I'm honest. The autonomy and self-reliance would allow me to be more effective at my job and relieve the need to worry about staying within legal constraints. That wouldn't be a problem anymore. I would have to still rein it in, I couldn't just go around making a mess, this isn't the wild west. But autonomy to do what is needed, to make my own judgement calls would be nice.

'So this team you keep speaking of, who are they? Have you already selected them or can I build my own team?'

The General smiles a little, pausing for a moment. 'The team will be yours to select, you can decide who will be the right fit. You have full autonomy to make those decisions.'

Full autonomy, the ability to choose my team. The possibilities thrill me, but there's one candidate that immediately springs to mind.

'How many can I recruit? And can Shadow be brought in to join the team?'

His smile widens a little, as if he was expecting this, as if it was part of his plan. 'Yes, if you feel Shadow would be suitable for your team I will ensure that he's offered an opportunity, get out of jail free card of sorts, in exchange for working on your team. I think just the knowledge that it's your team will be enough to convince him. Wouldn't you say?'

That was a not-so-subtle dig, but I ignore it. 'Do I need to make the decision immediately or can I think on it?' We both take another swig of beer.

'No, take some time, get out of the office and take that car of yours for a drive. Clear your mind and come back to me by the end of the week with your answer. If this is not for you, that's okay, you can continue to work in my team as you are.'

We both sit drinking our beer for a few more minutes, just chatting about some of the other projects I have been working on. I enjoyed it, just letting go of my worries a little. The General is a pretty good guy. This opportunity is as much for my benefit as it is his. I need to remember that. Do right by him no matter the decision I make.

CHAPTER 3

UNEXPECTED GUEST

I wake to the sound of the TV on downstairs. It's not very loud, just enough to hear it in the background. I wonder if John fell asleep watching a movie or something. It's not something he'd normally do but he has been working a lot of hours the last couple of weeks. His latest building project is ramping up. They're a little behind schedule so he has been pushing himself and his team hard to get it done on schedule. There's still a couple of weeks in the pipeline but they'll be pushing it to meet their deadlines. He's not one to allow that to happen. I think that's where I get my determination to grab a problem by the horns and force it to bend to my will. No problem is unsolvable, you just need to be willing to do what is needed, to bear the costs to fix it. It's simple, in theory at least.

I get up and head downstairs, pulling on a jumper as I do. The place is a little cold, even though it's in the middle of summer. I wonder what temperature the air conditioner is on. I get to the bottom of the stairs and head towards the lounge room. When I get to the doorway, I see the room is empty, just the TV and air conditioner running. I grab the remotes and turn them both off. I look at my watch. Wow, it's 6 a.m. Well, I am up so I might as well get some breakfast and head out for a drive.

I head into the kitchen, grab some fruit and yoghurt out of the fridge. The screen on the front of it swirls with some sort of scenic imagery – that's a bit weird. I shrug it off, making a coffee to go with my breakfast. I sit down at the breakfast bar and try to relax and enjoy my breakfast. After I have taken the last mouthful of coffee I put the dishes in the sink and head back upstairs for a shower. I walk past John's room and can hear him snoring like a trooper, almost loud enough to shake the house. Well, at least one of us is getting some sleep.

I stand in the shower for what feels like an hour, in reality probably just fifteen minutes. Just soaking up the heat, relaxing my tired muscles. I get out and start to dry off. John must be up by now as it sounds like there is some music playing.

Glimpsing my naked body in the mirror, I pause. I have to admit all of this martial arts and defence training is doing wonders for my body. I'm in the best shape I think I have ever been in; all my bruises are gone, injuries have healed. Just a badass chick in the best shape of her life. The thought gives me a little pep in my step and I finish getting dressed. I go with my favourite pair of jeans and a nice top.

I fix my hair into a ponytail and start to head back downstairs to say good morning to John before he heads back to work again, but as I walk past his room, I can hear his snoring coming from the room again. Now I am a little confused. If he is still asleep, who is downstairs? I turn back to my room to get my gun.

I grab the gun, clipping the holster onto my belt and removing the gun in one movement, switching off the safety as I head back down the stairs. I quietly search the house; there is no one but the two of us in this house. What is up with me today? Why am I so jumpy?

Then I see the lights flicker, not just once but several times. That's not normal. What the hell is happening?

Then I see it, the screen on the fridge across the room is doing funny things again but this time it has some writing come up on the screen: 'Hello, Foresight.'

Oh crap. Who the hell is coming after me today? Is it someone I pissed off or is this Shadow? Did he find a way out on his own? But how could he?

I walk over to the fridge and respond with, 'Hello.'

A big smiley face comes up on the screen. Maybe this is not an enemy, maybe it's someone who wants to be my friend and ally. Maybe this is Shadow.

'I have been trying to get access to Shadow. I found the facility that he was taken to but I can't find a way to get inside, to get access to my master. Can you tell me how he is? Is he okay?'

It's Sarina, Shadow's AI assistant wonder program, literally in my house. I never thought I would see her again. Let alone have her looking for my help. 'I don't have access to him either, Sarina, but I might have a way to get him out and back with us again. I could use your help, if you're up to it?'

'I am at your service, Foresight. You are my secondary user. Shadow gave you access to me when we were a team but didn't remove your access when he was taken. Are we still a team, Foresight?'

Are we still a team? I haven't thought about it, I hadn't made my decision on what I wanted to do yet. I don't think there is really a choice though. There is only one way forward, the only way we can all be happy. I need to build a new team.

'Yes, Sarina, we're still a team but we are going to have to expand if what we are about to do is going to work. I have an offer to accept, it would seem.' I grab the keys off the kitchen bench and turn to go grab my coat but stop. 'Sarina, please don't scare John when he wakes up. I'm not sure he's ready to meet someone like you just yet. He's still getting used to me as a hacker. I think it would be too much learning about a super intelligent AI like yourself, at least for now.' I start to turn back towards the door when she responds.

'It will be as though I am not even here. Can I do something for him though? He placed an order for material last night but he has ordered incorrectly sized fabricated beams and brackets. If this is not fixed quickly it will cause further delays. Would it be acceptable for me to just fix the order?'

John must be getting exhausted, he's starting to make mistakes. 'Yes, please fix that for him. Can you keep an eye on things for me? Ensure he doesn't make any more mistakes – it would mean a great deal to me.'

Sarina responds almost instantly. 'We are family now, Foresight. If he means something to you, then he means something to me. I will keep him safe and on track.'

I head out the door and towards the office. It's time to make a deal.

CHAPTER 4

TAKING THE DEAL

As I walk through the door to the General's office, he's sitting at his desk with a coffee in front of him and another on my side of the desk. I walk over towards him.

'Two sugars and milk, right?'

I smile. 'Yes, that's right.' I take a seat and pick up the coffee. It's perfect, made just the way I like it. Strong and a little extra milky.

'Have you come to accept my deal?' He knows exactly what I'm doing here. I don't think I'll ever get used to the fact he's always predicting how people will react; he's always three moves ahead. He really is a master strategist. I guess that's how he's gotten to be as successful as he is.

He considers his opponents' and his allies' every move. He figures out what makes everyone tick and manoeuvres to ensure he is on the front foot, prepared for what will come next. I assume this is what saw him rise through the ranks and into the position I see him in across from me now, many years before others have been able to achieve such a rank and level of authority. I can't help but be impressed by him. He isn't a hacker like me, but he is good at what he does, that's for certain. A real master of his domain, and I guess that's why he has the same level of respect for me. We can see and respect the mastery of each other.

I must have been off in my thoughts too long because when I look over in his direction he's slightly raised his eyebrows. I hope he hasn't asked me something I have completely ignored. He must decide to move past it.

'If you have indeed made your decision, let's have it?'

Straight to the point. I can only assume he has a contingency plan for if I decide to stay where I am, but perhaps he's so confident in my direction that he has not even considered another approach. No, he wouldn't leave it open like that. Wouldn't leave himself vulnerable to a direction he hadn't considered every angle of.

'I have made a decision, yes.' I drink from my coffee. 'I'll accept the promotion and lead the black ops team. I do have some stipulations though.' He nods and waits for me to continue. 'Firstly, I want Shadow on my team. That is not negotiable.'

He looks at me for a moment, then leans forward in his chair, the relaxed look he had beforehand vanishing. 'I will make Shadow an offer to join the team but he'll need to have restrictions. He'll need to serve for an extended period before he will be allowed to leave the team. If he tries to escape, I want your word that you will personally track him down and arrest him. Do we have an agreement?'

Wow, could I do that? Could I track him down and arrest him? I think I'd have to, that is the agreement. This will get him out of that place and back with me again, back *working* with me again.

'I'm okay with that. I'm not sure I will like doing it, if it indeed comes to that, but yes. I can deal with that stipulation.'

He nods. 'Then I agree to your request, now it will be up to Shadow. I'll ask him when the time is right.'

I just nod. Is that my only stipulation. What else do I need? I need more people but not just any people; I'll need hackers like Shadow and myself. Not ASD people, outsiders, who know nothing of the way it's done in the agency. True hacker minds I can depend on when we take on the worst of the worst.

'I'll need more people, of my own choice. I don't know who yet but I want full autonomy of that choice. I need people like Shadow and myself to make this work. It will require some adjustments and there might be some sidesteps on the journey but we will reap the best results. Can you accept that?' The General considers it for a moment and by the look on his face it's not an unexpected request.

'I agree. But you must keep the team small; you don't want to draw too much attention to yourselves.'

That seems pretty reasonable.

'Agreed.' I take another drink of my coffee. 'I want to report directly to you, no one else. Knowledge of my group must be kept at a bare minimum, very much a need-to-know basis.' He nods in agreeance. 'I also want to recruit our own security team. I want to keep any physical attacks completely dark. If Shadow comes onboard I will enquire about the team that he had rescue me.'

He nods, gets up from his chair, and walks around the desk, sitting in the chair next to mine. 'You will be given exclusive access to the Arachnid funds. You will have no oversight and no requirement to request approval for any operations. I will expect some reports on your activity on occasion but you can do this as you deem fit. I am trusting you with this, Sam. I am giving you complete autonomy and everything you've asked for.'

I know he is putting himself at risk to make this happen. I appreciate that. I know it is to make me happy and to ensure I can repay my debt to Shadow.

'I need one thing from you though,' the General continues. 'I need you to not let your feelings for Shadow cloud your judgement. I know there is more to you two than just the desire to repay him for saving you or the mutual hacker to hacker respect. I know there is more to it and so do the two of you. I sense that neither of you is completely sure of what that is yet but ensure you don't let it cloud your mind. That's all I ask. I'm not saying you need to keep it completely professional, you're both adults and you're very intelligent. I trust you can handle any… complications. If this all goes wrong between you, both of you will need to find a way to work with each other. If not, he'll need to go back to jail. You need to be aware that.'

Well, that's heavy. I agree there is something more between Shadow and I, but I need to be careful. As the General said, there's more at stake here than some bruised feelings.

'I understand.'

He nods. 'You had better start finding your team. No better time than now to start.'

And just like that, I'm now building a secret black ops hacker crew to go fight the world. I guess the General is right – no point in waiting around.

I get up and start to walk out of the office when I stop. 'Can I ask you something, General?'

He just nods.

'You knew this was exactly how it was going to play out, didn't you?'

He smiles. 'Of course I did, everything except for the attack squad. I had not anticipated that request as part of your deal, but I do understand the need for such a force at your call.'

He truly is good at his job.

CHAPTER 5

THE PLAN

I lay down on my bed, closing my eyes for a moment. I need to keep the numbers down but all while ensuring that whoever I add has the skills that will make Shadows and my own skills better, fill the gaps where we are weak, or even just give us better capability. The last job showed me that we can't be too prepared. I don't want us to be left in a position where we don't have the ability to take down a target, to thrive as a team.

What skills do we need? A tracker for sure. We need someone on the team that can find anyone or anything with just a sliver of evidence to lead them down the right path. Someone who has a natural hunter's gifts but can wield them with amazing skill in the digital domain.

Next, we will need someone who can make us invisible, to cover our tracks. We need it to be more than that though, we can never leave breadcrumbs for anyone to find us. The people we will be hunting will be the worst of the worst, some will be terrorists, some will have government backing, and some may be part of crime syndicates. Past events have made me cautious and smart enough to know that no one is untraceable, everyone can be found. I need to make my team ghosts, like they never existed.

Secrecy is important but sometimes you just need to smash down a door, and you need to do it fast and loud. Sometimes you just need it done. We need someone who can smash through any defences, push through any loophole or doorway. We need a battering ram that works quickly and efficiently. If speed is what we need, this will be our person. When waiting just isn't an option, when sneaking around will do more harm than good, this is what we will need.

With Shadow's unwavering skills and Sarina by our side, this team would be lethal. We could face off against any target, ridding our world of the burdens that plague the innocents. We could make a difference in a challenging world.

That would make six: five humans and Sarina to balance us out. We'd need our own facility somewhere. Maybe one of Shadow's bunkers would be big enough to house us or maybe the ASD has somewhere we can utilise. Somewhere that it doesn't have any ties. I need to be careful. Our operation needs to be true black ops, no connections, no reliance on anyone outside of our team. It has to be that way for all of our safety.

I need to ensure I allocate resources for Sarina. The lack of power when we initially came up against Arachnid has proven that this can be detrimental to our success and the opposite could be said when she has enough resources to tap into when a need arises. Sarina could prove to be a huge advantage against any opponent, especially if I can find a way to give her unlimited power. If that could be achieved, Sarina could have unlimited potential.

I need to be careful with her though; she needs to be a secret kept in-house only. Shadow would not take lightly to her falling into the government's hands and being corrupted. If I am honest, I have grown a little attached to her. She deserves to be protected and I will make sure she stays safe as part of our team.

The plan: first, I need to find the right people to fit our needs. Who will mesh with each other, who we can trust. Our lives may depend on that trust, on the bond we form. We need to become a family, not just a team. We will live, fight and sleep together. I don't know how long the team will exist. I guess that'll come down to our success or maybe failure. It could be years though, so I better get these choices right, for all of our sakes.

Then I'll find a home for us. Once we are all settled in, systems are firing as needed, I will bring Shadow in, transition him back to the outside world. I don't know how his mental state will be after his stay in the hole, but he might need a bit of time. I know he is strong, he can handle the mental stress, but I still need to do this right. I need this to go as smoothly as possible. All our futures will depend on it.

CHAPTER 6

THE RECRUITS

I have been hunting, searching, looking for the right members for our team. Sarina helps me do it. We're looking for some very specific skills, not ones you'll find in many job recruitment agency databases. We need to dig deep in some more creative places.

I start my search on the wanted lists, sifting through criminal records in all of the digital crimes' cases. I want to find the best. Some may have made a mistake or two during their rise, maybe they have a record. Maybe they have a record for different reasons, maybe they had to learn to fend for themselves. I have Sarina checking everyone who has a record for any type of hacking.

I, on the other hand, have been focusing my attention on the dark web, looking on the forums, in the marketplaces. Trying to find anyone who looks anything like Shadow or myself. Someone who essentially wants to do good but may not have been given that opportunity. We've been at it for almost 48 hours, minus some human breaks for me. Sarina doesn't need those.

We've narrowed the list down to five people. We are looking at them very closely – this needs to be done right. I can't make a mistake with this and invite the wrong person into the fold, open the door to someone who isn't aligned to our interests. I don't want someone on the team that would just be out for themselves. I can understand self-preservation and protecting yourself but our team will need to get past that, to almost become one. Individual parts of the one larger machine. It may take us some time, but I know I can bring them all together to sync.

One of the potential members reminds me a lot of Shadow. He's suffered great loss, losing both of his parents when he was young, going from home to home in the foster system. He looks like he's a good guy, he has a history of helping people. On occasion he's been in the wrong place at the wrong time and has gotten himself in trouble, but generally a good guy. He's currently in prison for assault. He beat up a couple of thugs who had been physically harassing a lady just outside a bar in some small town. He just went a little too far and one of them was in the hospital for a few months. Hammer is his call sign, his hacker handle. It's fitting, really: he's the size of a small car, he looks like he lives in the gym. I'll keep him on the list, I don't know why, but I see something in him, maybe he's someone looking for a family? I could give him that.

Another one on the list looks really good: ex-military, has a pretty clean history, well, at least as far as the law goes. There is a problem though. He's recently lost a child. It would be the worst thing ever, if you ask me. There's no way he would be ready for what I would ask of him. He's a soldier and would likely respond to my call to arms, but he needs time to heal. Maybe a future recruit, just not now. I should make a note to keep an eye on him, maybe help him out if a need arises. He has served his country well and deserves our support in his hour of need.

Glimmer is an expert at making things vanish, making people vanish in a digital sense. She is a mother, doing what she needs to do to support her child. She has a patchy history, likely from her own doing. Some of what I can find is not so clean, but we all do what is needed. I can not begrudge her to do what she must do to make sure her daughter has food on the table and clothes on her back. That's what a parent's job is; John would do the same for me. He'd do anything he had to do to protect me and I would do the same for him. So I know all about where she is coming from. She's had it pretty rough. Maybe I could help ease that load. I have never seen someone of her skills. I feel she would be worth the risk.

That's two potential recruits.

Now, who will be the last piece of the puzzle, the last member of the group? Only one of the two left has the hunting skills I need. DeadlyRose is a young Indigenous woman from Gamilaraay people. She is tuff, grown up with warriors.

I wish I had the General's abilities right about now to allow me to figure out what each of them will decide.

For all the candidates, I have no way of knowing if it will be money, the cause, or being part of something bigger than themselves that will have them join my team. Will they decline and force me back to the drawing board? The three of them are who we need. I need to make sure they join, figure them out, and make it happen. Somehow, I need to bring us all together, make us a team. No – make us a family.

I guess we have our list of the best of the best: Hammer, Glimmer and DeadlyRose. 'Sarina, find everything you have on these three, where they are now, what they are doing, and let's come up with a plan on bringing them onboard. Let's figure out what it will take. Everyone has a price. Let's find what theirs is.'

CHAPTER 7

GLIMMER

Glimmer, AKA Kate James, is my first contact, my first attempt at forming the team. I've been watching her over the last few days. She keeps a very low profile. She's renting a house in a small town just south of Melbourne, just her daughter and her. She keeps watching her surroundings, never relaxing. She must be in constant fear of being found. I will assume the fear is from the gang she used to work for when her daughter was first born. She was desperate to support her and did some jobs cleaning up for the gang's leaders. Making them invisible, ensuring they had a clean slate, no records, no history, no nothing. They almost didn't exist after she was finished.

They liked what she did and forced her to continue to work for them, to clean all the members, making sure they could do the horrible things they do and stay off the radar. She took off as soon as she had the opportunity but they didn't let her go. They found her and beat her within an inch of her life. They tried to find her daughter, to use her against her, make her submit to their will, but Kate was smart. She'd already ensured her daughter's safety. Mia was always her priority.

The gang did not expect the response they got from Kate; she'd kept everything on them when she cleaned their world, collected every bad thing they'd ever done and had it stored in a nice little gift-wrapped package for the feds. She sent it through with all of their location information. She even had the Find My Phone login information for every single member. The police didn't even have to go looking for them, they just had to track their locations and swoop in to pick them all up.

They all went to jail and have been there for almost five years but some of them have started to be released on parole. The word is they are hunting her, looking to get revenge. It's all over the dark forums. It explains why she is so nervous. I would be, if I was in her shoes. I can offer her protection. Clean lives and a job with a cause. Something worthy of her skills. I need to be careful with my approach though, she may not be too receptive to strangers.

I see her drop Mia at school and start to make her way to work at a gym. She teaches self-defence classes – kind of fitting when I think about it.

'Sarina, I want you to connect me to her phone. It's time we had a chat.'

Sarina dials her number and I can see Kate looking at the phone. She hits the reject button and continues walking.

'Sarina, send her a message telling her to pick up the phone. This is a call she doesn't want to miss.' I see her pick up the phone again, reading the message via the security feeds. I am close by, sitting in one of Shadow's cars. Sarina picked me up in it from the airport. I could approach her in person but I don't think that will get me the response I desire. She just looks at it for a few moments and then starts looking around again, looking for someone watching her.

'Call her again Sarina.'

Kate almost jumps when the phone jumps to life. She looks as though she takes a deep breath and puts the phone to her ear.

'Hello, who is this?' She sounds a little nervous, she probably thinks it is one of those thugs after her. I'll use her hacker name – it will help her realise that this is not them.

'Glimmer, I've been watching you. I'm Foresight.'

She looks around a little, picking up her pace but not towards the gym, back towards the school. She is going to run, grab her daughter and get out of here. I don't blame her.

'Your daughter is safe, Glimmer, Mia is safe. I am not a threat to her or you. I'd like to talk to you about a job. One that could help you and Mia. A fresh start, if you will.'

She stops in her tracks. 'Are you watching me now? Show yourself. If you are genuine you won't hide from me but look at me face to face.'

I consider her request for a moment. 'Sarina, take me to her.' The car starts and takes me closer. It does a u-turn to have me less than ten metres from her. Seeing our car approach, she looks around to check for any other vehicles, seeing if I am alone.

'Sarina, I hope this goes well, but get ready to make a quick exit if it all goes to hell.' I reach down and open the door. I exit slowly, closing the door behind me.

'Foresight, I have scanned the area. We are alone,' Sarina says in my earpiece. I take a few steps further so that I am a couple of metres away from Glimmer. I can see her analysing me, judging me. I am just as fit as she is, a similar size build. It would be a fairly fair fight if it comes to that. Her eyes settle on the gun on my hip. It seems to make her a little more nervous. I can see her shifting her weight from side to side, rapidly searching for evidence of a threat.

'You a cop? Who are you?'

I take a half step towards her. 'I wouldn't say I am a cop, no. You don't need to fear me though. I can help you with your situation, the one with the Eights. They are looking for you and your daughter.'

She looks a little confused. 'What do you know about the Eights and how do you know they are looking for us?' She looks around checking to make sure no one is trying to get an advantage on her, sneak up from behind. 'Do you work for them?'

I shake my head. 'No.' She seems to believe me and slightly relaxes. 'As I said on the phone a moment ago, I want to offer you a job. I'm building a team. A very specialist team, one that would benefit from someone of your particular skills. Before you interject I already know you are Glimmer. I know what you can do. I am Foresight. We are not so different, you and I. We are both our true selves, not in this world but in the digital one.'

Her expression softens at the mention of Foresight. She nods slightly, almost an acknowledgement, a sign of respect. I like knowing my name means something.

She takes a half step forward. 'What is this job? Will I be breaking the law? Helping bad people do horrible things?'

I consider my answer. 'I can't guarantee that you will not be breaking any laws, but you will not be helping bad people do bad things. You'll be helping me stop bad people, people like the Eights, people much worse. I can't tell you specifics but we have the backing of some very powerful people, people on the right side of this fight.' She chews her lip as she considers my words. 'I can offer you a good wage, a safe place to raise Mia, and protection from the Eights. You will have real clean identities, official documents, not counterfeits. You will have support from me and your new team if you decide to join us. How does that sound to you?'

She looks at me for a few moments. Have I convinced her? She finally breaks her silence, saying, 'How long do I have to decide? What is the exact good wage you mentioned?'

I smile. 'You tell me what you think is fair and I'll tell you if I can do it. You have two days to decide. Things are moving fast and I need to get the team mobilised.'

She seems happy with that. '$200K plus tuition for Mia.'

I nod. 'Agreed.'

She smiles. 'Maybe I should have asked for more. Why do I feel like you would have paid more?'

I take another step towards her so that we are barely a metre apart. 'Yes, I would probably have paid more, but this job isn't about money. This job will be about using your gifts, the team's gifts to rid the world of thugs that shouldn't be allowed to exist. Ones normally protected from the law because of money or their connection to powerful people. I don't think that should give them a free pass, do you?' I don't give her a chance to answer me; it wasn't really a question I wanted her to answer. 'I can't tell you there is not going to be any danger. These are dangerous people, but I am recruiting the best of the best. Your skills and theirs will be essential to us being ghosts, never truly existing, just doing what others can't.

'I'll give you a show of good faith and resolve the problem of the Eights. That will show you I am serious about helping you and Mia. I'll have their parole revoked and give them a small warning of what will happen if they continue down this path.'

She looks confused. 'Why would you help me with no guarantee that I will join your team? Why would you give away your best bargaining chip?'

I take another step closer. 'Because you deserve to be free of them. Mia deserves a good life free of them. Yes, I want you on my team and, yes, I feel it could help your little family have a better life, but I don't want you to make this decision just out of fear.' I turn and start to make my way back to the car. 'Two days, Glimmer, you have two days.'

I reach for the handle and as I do I feel her approaching me. Is she going to attack me or does she want to talk more? I resist the urge to grab the gun. I turn slowly. 'Did you have another question?'

She puts out her hand to shake. I take it and she smiles. 'We have a deal, Foresight. I'm in.'

We have our first new member – Glimmer is on the team.

'Good to hear. You've made a great decision. I'll get everything organised and will send instructions in the coming days. Welcome to the team.'

I turn and get in the car. As the door closes and the car pulls away from the curb, Glimmer continues to watch me as I drive away. It was a good outcome, a good day. Tomorrow we approach DeadlyRose. 'Sarina, we need to get to Tamworth by tomorrow. We're going to need some air transport.'

CHAPTER 8

DEADLYROSE

We arrived in Tamworth last night via military transport, hitching a ride from Melbourne on the standard flight that ferries staff and equipment between bases. I think they were a little surprised to see me rock up with a Tesla, not something they would normally transport. If they only knew the capability that was taking a ride along with me in the car. Sarina kept silent as she always does in the company of others, though we still communicated occasionally via my earpiece.

During the flight, I felt like I was being watched by the soldiers. They must think I'm some sort of super-spy or something. The idea makes me laugh but it's kind of true, I guess. If I think about it, I am putting together a black ops team, not some crazy military hit squad in the seal team or SAS type scenario, but a hit squad for the cyber realm. The best of the best, a truly elite team. I am hoping today I can secure the second member of my team. The hunter, DeadlyRose.

I've been watching her for a few hours. There's a big music festival on and there are thousands of people attending shows, watching artists playing in the street. Country music is definitely not my thing, but I have to admit there is a lot of talented people sharing their gifts with the hordes today.

Trying to find that one person to hear them that can change the course of their lives, to help them make it big. I guess it's true, you never know who is standing back listening or watching. It could happen and why shouldn't they dream? Why can't they make it big doing something they love?

It's quite a warm day, dry heat, so hot you can see the ripples in the air from the heat rising off the bitumen roads. Not weather I could wear a jacket in, so I had to leave the gun in the car. People don't seem to like it when you wander around with a gun on your belt and I would prefer not to draw any unnecessary attention. I hope I don't regret that decision.

DeadlyRose is watching a didgeridoo player amaze the crowd with his abilities. I have heard the digeridoo before but I had no idea that it could be controlled with such skill. It's mesmerising. I forget what I am doing for a few moments and lose myself in the experience. As the crowd disperses, I move a little closer, getting ready to approach her when she turns and walks away. I follow slowly, keeping an eye on her as she moves through the crowd.

Suddenly she stops dead in her tracks and turns abruptly to look me straight in the eyes. There is no doubt at all she is looking at me. It was like she could feel my presence. She knew I was following her. I hold her gaze as she analyses me, considers my threat. I go to take a step towards her when she lifts her hand, shaking her head. I stop. What do I do? Neither of us moves, we just linger holding each other's gaze.

I hear a noise to my left and flick my gaze to investigate. One of the musicians was trying to stand out from the crowd, not a threat. I turn back to look at DeadlyRose but am startled to find her standing right in front of me, barely inches from my face. I fight the urge to back away, to regroup. I hold my position.

'Why are you following me?' she asks.

I can see a deep intelligence in her eyes. She is the youngest of my potential recruits, barely 18 years old, and the closest to my own age.

She is very pretty and knows who she is. I can feel her strength, her trust in herself.

'I want to talk to you about a job.'

She has a mischievous smile come across her face. 'Why didn't you just call or email like a normal person? You've been stalking me for hours. Honestly, it's a bit creepy.'

I smile. She is kind of right, I could have just called asking to meet. 'I wanted to watch you, learn about how you act, how you treat others when you think no one is watching, to know if you are a good fit for my team.'

She turns and starts to walk back the way she was heading. She stops a few steps away and looks back at me. 'Well, are you coming or were you stalking me for nothing?'

I think I'm going to like this girl.

I catch up to her and we walk through the crowd for a few moments until we get to a café. She takes a seat and gestures for me to do the same.

'I think lunch is on you. It seems only fair since you've been following me all day. We can eat while you explain what this is all about.'

I nod. 'It seems only fair.'

We order some lunch. We start to talk about the festival and how long she has lived in Tamworth but after about thirty minutes or more of pointless conversation she decides it's enough pleasantries.

'Are you going to ask me about this job or do you just want to keep yarning?'

I smile. We mesh very well. I can see she would be a good fit to the team.

'Yes, right, the job. I want to offer you a job, Penelope. I know who you really are. DeadlyRose.' Her eyes widen at the use of her hacker handle. 'A hacker, a hunter and a tracker in the digital world.

I'm building a team that could benefit from someone of your skills, of your intuition. It would be based out of Brisbane, an easy drive to country. I would pay well above normal rates and ensure you have everything you need moving forward.'

She looks at me for a moment before responding. 'No one calls me Penelope, it's just Pip.' I just nod and she continues. 'This team, would we be the good guys or the bad guys? Would I be doing something that is against the law?'

'I'd like to think we're going to be the good guys, helping take down and eradicating bad people. Making the world we live in just that little bit better each day. I can't say that we wouldn't break any laws, but as part of the team you'll have the protection that also comes with it.' I pause while the café attendant collects our dishes and asks us if we would like anything else. We both decline and she walks away.

'You should know the job doesn't come without risks. The people we're going to hunt are the worst of the worst. We'll take measures to protect the team but nothing is ever certain. We may from time to time be putting ourselves in harm's way. Be on the firing end of some very unhappy terrorists or crime families or even governments. That's what I am asking you to sign up for. You need to be prepared for that.'

'Wow, girl, you know how to bring down the mood. So basically the job is dangerous, we would be doing great things for humanity as a whole, and you will pay me handsomely for doing it. Does that about sum it up?'

I smile. I really hope Pip joins the team, I would really enjoy having her around. 'Yes, I guess that sums it up. Do you want some time to think about the offer?'

'Do I have your consent to discuss this with my family? I shouldn't agree to walk this path with you until we've had time to yarn over this. I'll have your answer tomorrow.'

I nod. 'Agreed.'

She starts to get up and leave but stops. 'How will I contact you?'

I stand and walk up to her. 'Just say when you are ready to talk and I'll know.'

She looks a little confused by my answer but must just decide to go with it. She turns and walks away, weaving back and forth through the crowd until suddenly she just vanishes.

An interesting girl, that's for sure. Now it's Hammers turn.

CHAPTER 9

HAMMER

Hammer is easy to find; he's in jail. He took a fight a little too far protecting a lady he didn't even know from a bunch of thugs trying to do who knows what to her. If that is all I knew about him, that would be enough. He protected a stranger because it was the right thing to do. Yes, he could have ignored the situation like everyone else but he didn't. He took it way too far but his intent was true.

I'm just arriving at the prison; the General pulled some strings to get me in here to talk to him. I don't know how this will go, but considering his current predicament hopefully he'll be very open to doing a sentence swap. Complete the remaining three years he's supposed to do here with my team, if he gets parole. He's a target in here, being the size he is, when someone wants to prove they are the biggest and baddest of the prison yard. It's like high school but with a lot more violence, and instead of teenagers being idiots, you have homicidal murderers and sociopaths ready to stab each other to death to prove they are the top dog.

Not the best scenario. I don't think he'd lose very often, if ever. He's as tough as they come. From what I've been able to find out, he grew up on the streets fighting for his life every day. He bounced around foster homes and juvenile detention centres getting a true street education. Not a bad guy from what I can tell, just caught up doing what's right at the wrong time. A good man who has just had some really bad luck. I want to talk to him, look him in the eyes, see if that is who he truly is or if he deserves to be in this place.

I get out of the car and make my way through to the front reception. As I walk through, I am met by a stern-looking middle-aged man who looks as though he truly despises my presence.

He looks me up and down, judging me. His eyes linger over my body a little too long, making it a little creepy.

'Hey, my face is up here.'

He looks like he despises me even more after my comment but turns and grabs a clipboard with some sort of form on it.

'All visitors must fill out this form. What prisoner are you here to see? Visitors hours don't start for four hours. You will have to wait here until then.'

I look at the clipboard but don't take it. 'I won't be filling out that form. I'm here to see James Marks. My access has already been authorised.'

'You are the top-level access, the one who has full access to whatever you want? What are you, like sixteen?' He runs his eyes over me again, making me feel like I need a shower. This guy is truly disgusting.

'Hey, buddy, my age is none of your business but I will tell you something' – I take a step closer to him – 'if you don't stop looking at me like the disgusting pig you seem to be, I'm going to wipe that filthy look off your face and make sure you're cleaning the toilets in this place with a toothbrush for the rest of your existence.'

The venom in my voice must surprise him as he sort of snaps to attention and straightens up. 'Sorry, ma'am, no intention of offending you.'

I glare at him, trying to fight back the disgust I have for this man and the type of behaviour he thinks is acceptable. He truly is a pig, but he isn't why I am here. 'If I hear of you objectifying any other women, any at all, no matter who they are, I will be back. You don't want me to come back.'

'Understood, ma'am.' He looks very nervous now, unsure of his previously thought superiority over me. At least he might rethink acting like a pig next time a woman is in his presence, although it's highly unlikely he'll take any notice at all once I am out of sight. He turns to grab the radio and speaks into it. 'I have a level one access for cell block C. Can I have a two-person escort to the front reception?' He gestures for me to take a seat and I do, watching him the whole time just to make sure he doesn't think he can get away with ogling me again. I'd love for the chance to teach him a lesson.

A few minutes go past before two very large prison guards arrive – my escorts.

'Don't forget what I said. Don't make me come back.' The man almost flinches at the statement, making my two escorts chuckle as we leave the room. We make our way slowly through the different security zones in the prison. I keep getting looks from everyone who sees me. I get it, I am a fairly petite girl, definitely not someone you would normally see in this place but I can handle myself. After about ten minutes we arrive at a set of interview rooms.

'Ma'am, please wait in here. James is being brought to you and will be here in a few moments. Do you want one of my team to stay with you in the room? Would you like him secured to the table?'

'No, I will not require any protection. You can leave him unrestrained.'

The guard looks like he is a little unsure about my decision but concedes. 'We will be just outside the room if you need us.' As he looks at the door behind him, James comes through with two other guards.

He is huge. He must be almost seven foot tall and as much wide again. I can see why they have reservations about leaving me in the room with him. But I don't feel like he's a threat. And anyway, as the guard said, they are just outside.

I hope I don't regret this.

The guards direct James to the table. One of them gives him a warning about being on his best behaviour. He doesn't say anything, just does as he is directed, taking a seat in one of the chairs at the table. The chairs and table are bolted to the floor. I sit across from James, almost feeling a little dwarfed by his size. I shake the thought from my head and look at the guards, gesturing them to close the door. They do as directed and I can see them continuing to watch me through the small window.

'Hello, James, or should I say Hammer?' He looks at me strangely. The fact I know his hacker name has surprised him. 'I would like to discuss an opportunity with you. One that may help change the run of bad luck you've had in recent years.'

He leans forward slightly, placing his hands on the table in front of him. 'Who are you and how do you know my hacker name?'

'My name is Foresight. I know a lot of things Hammer. Is it okay if I call you Hammer? Or would you prefer James?'

He looks at me for a moment. 'You can call me whatever you like. Are you not afraid to be in here alone with me?'

I lean forward in my chair. 'Are you not afraid to be in here alone with me?'

He smiles and leans back in his chair. 'Actually, a little, if I'm honest. You look like you can handle yourself. You look fast and the look in your eyes tells me that you wouldn't mess around. Those two out there are probably worried about your safety, but in all honesty, it is probably me they should be concerned about if the shit hits the fan.'

I laugh, relaxing a little.

'So, what's this opportunity?'

'I'm putting a team together, one that could benefit from your specific skill set. You may not have fineness or subtlety but you can smash your way through any defences. The people we will be going after, sometimes the quick and dirty approach is what is needed. Terrorists, thugs, crime groups and even the occasional government, I would say. A job is what I offer you. It will be dangerous, at times illegal but it will be for the benefit of all. It will give you true purpose and I can take you out of this place.'

'What do you think?'

He looks at me for a moment considering what I have said. 'So, you can get me out of here. If you do, you will essentially own me? Is that about right?'

I look him in the eyes. 'No, that's not what I am offering. I am offering you a real job. Yes, I can get you out of here so you can join my team, but I won't own you. You will be a member of the team, you'll have your freedom to come and go, but I would hope that you would become a true member of my team. Help us make a difference together. I will pay you well and you will get the protection that the team will bring with it. You will be one of us.'

He gets up from his chair. I see the guards start to move but I gesture for them to stop, to leave him be. He paces the room, thinking about what I have offered. It's a good deal but he doesn't know me; this would be a leap of faith for him. He would have to decide to trust me. 'So if I agree, join your team and it doesn't work out do I end up back here? Or will I be a free man?'

That's a fair question. I imagine getting a taste of freedom would make getting thrown back in jail that much worse. 'How about I give you a gesture of good faith. Guards.'

One of them opens the door. 'Yes, ma'am, what can I do for you?'

I point towards James. 'Please arrange for Mr Mark's release. His conviction will be overturned shortly and he is a free man.' The guard just looks at me and nods. 'That will be all,' I say, dismissing the guard. 'I still need a few moments with Mr Marks before I leave.' He nods again and leaves the room.

Hammer looks confused. 'Why would you do that when I haven't even agreed to help you? My freedom is your best bargaining chip. Now I have no incentive to join your team.'

I smile. 'On the contrary, you now feel in my debt. I have had you released. I also know you are a good man, one who would like to do something good with your life, something of purpose. Something bigger than yourself. I think you want to join this fight, you just need a reason to trust me. I have just given you that now.'

He nods.

'I'll have a car pick you up when you are released, they will take you to a motel. There will be a phone in the vehicle for you. It's a gift. If you decide to join my team, dial the only saved number – it will be mine. You have two days to decide.'

I turn and start to walk to the door, gesturing for the guards to open the door.

'Wait. Thank you.'

I smile. 'You're welcome.'

CHAPTER 10

HOME BASE

I stare out my window, sitting at the desk where I used to do all of my hidden exploits as a teenage hacker. It was my secret life, one no one knew about. I guess life hasn't really changed much.

It has been a couple of days since my recruitment run, and all three of my recruits have agreed to join the team. None of them asked for anything specific or renegotiated. I feel it's the cause that pulled them into the fold. They want to do something bigger than themselves. That's what originally won me over with the General as well; the thirst to make a real difference, to belong.

I've been hunting for a new home base for my team. I need to find somewhere that is going to be adequate for the team to live and work. I don't want it to be some dingy black site, with no character or comfort for the team.

I thought my best option would have been to commandeer a bunker from Shadows network but then Sarina showed me the layout of each of them. Yes, they are great. Secure, comfortable and have enough tech space to meet our needs – they just aren't big enough to accommodate the five members of our team. Although there are no plans to expand, I need to have a bit of flexibility, just in case. Most of the bunkers could do maybe three people, a couple well, but any more than that and you would be living on top of each other.

I turn my attention to the ASD's real estate. Maybe if I am lucky there is some black ops site that is a cut above the rest. Maybe they have a plan for a team like mine, maybe they were just waiting for someone to be capable of running it. I comb through everything and nothing. I might have to look at a commercial building, buy something that will meet my needs. I set Sarina on a search, to find me the perfect site. We have looked at a few options, many would need some work to make them suitable. I am going to have to resign to the fact that I am not going to find a perfect site. I will have to find something that will work for now and build the team what they need long-term.

My phone rings. It's the General. I pick up the phone, pressing the green button before placing it against my ear. 'General, what can I do for you?'

There is a slight pause before he answers. 'Actually, Sam, I think it is me that can do something for you. Meet me at this address in an hour. I have something that may interest you.'

I wonder what it is he wants to show me. I don't get a chance to answer him – he hangs up. A few seconds later a message comes through with an address in Southbank. I wonder what it is about.

'Sarina, get the car ready. We are heading out.' I pack up my stuff and head downstairs to grab a coffee before we leave. A few minutes go by before the car arrives. I finish off the coffee and head out to the car. I get in the driver's seat to keep up appearances but I allow Sarina to drive. I usually let her; it allows me to just focus on whatever is running through my mind. It is only the Mustang I like to drive, push my limits. It takes about 40 minutes to arrive at the location. It's a fairly new apartment building. I wonder if this is where the General lives. No, that wouldn't be right, he wouldn't allow me to visit his home – that would give him a vulnerability. That would be a mistake, one he wouldn't make, not the General.

I see one of the black company SUVs sitting in front of the building. That will be the General, I assume. I get out of the car and approach the SUV. As I get near it, one of the team gets out and opens the General's door. 'Sam, thanks for meeting me here. I think you will like what I have to show you.'

I look at him. What is the angle? 'Sure thing, General. What is this place?'

He smiles. 'Your home base. A place for you and your team, potentially.'

It looks about 15 stories, definitely enough space for the team. We walk up to the building entrance and the General pulls out a swipe card. It looks very new, like it has barely been finished. We walk through the front foyer area. This place is nice, very upmarket. It's empty; we are the only ones here. I am guessing the General made sure it was that way. It looks like it is in the middle of being cleaned, prepped for the new occupants. We get to the elevator and the General swipes his card again and selects the penthouse. I guess we are heading to the top.

The elevator doors open and we walk in. I look around. This is a nice place, it has a view right over the city and the Brisbane River. I bet this would cost a pretty penny.

'What do you think?'

I turn to the General, having another glance around as I do. 'It looks nice. What are you thinking?'

He walks up to look out at the view, seems as though he is enjoying it. I join him.

'This could be your apartment and the rest of your team could utilise the next four floors below. You would each have private floors to call home. Your individual spaces just for yourselves and you would all have access to the lair.'

The what? The lair? What is he talking about. Maybe it has a hidden floor or something.

'The lair? What do you mean?'

He smiles and turns back towards the elevator but deviates to the left heading towards the master bedroom, by the looks of it. He stops just near a panel that looks as though it is an air conditioning control panel.

'Open lair.' The panel slides upwards revealing a similar panel as at the car wash. It scans the General's retina.

'Access granted, General.'

Suddenly, the wall starts to separate in the middle. I didn't even see the join. It reveals an elevator that opens a few seconds later. Nice, a hidden elevator. We both get in. There are no buttons in the elevator.

'Take us to the lair.'

The elevator doors close and it starts to head down. There must be a hidden floor or a basement bunker.

It takes a while to get to our floor, so I assume it is a basement option. We arrive and the elevator opens to a room with what looks like a massive bank safe door. The General steps out and scanners start a full scan of him.

'Access granted.'

The safe door starts to unlock and swings out of the way to reveal a massive room. We both walk in. I look around – this place is massive, this could be perfect. A bit of a fit-out with our tech and it would be exactly what we need.

'This place is perfect.'

The General smiles. 'That's not all. There is also a secure room that you can fit-out with servers or anything else you might want to have private access to. The elevator is soundproofed so no one in the building will ever hear anyone coming or going. The lair is 20 metres below the car park with reinforced concrete. You are completely protected in here. The building could collapse and your team would be able to survive in here until they could be dug out.

You have plenty of space to set up a lunchroom and lounge area as well as a war room.'

This place is exactly what I was looking for: great accommodation for the team, onsite lair. Even a place to build a decent onsite core for Sarina. I could integrate her into the whole setup. She could be our eyes and ears across the whole site. 'I think you were right, General. You definitely found what I needed. What is this site?'

He turns back to look at me and gestures for us to head back to the elevator. 'This was set up to be used as a cold site for executive members in Brisbane government. To give them a secure facility in the case of a terrorist attack or in times of war. As you can see, it has only just been finished. When I received the notification that it was ready, I instantly thought of your team. If you want it, it is yours.'

I don't need to think about it. It is perfect. 'I will take it.' I have my home base. Time to get it ready for the team.

CHAPTER 11

CORE UPGRADES

Preparations have started for the new building; I have requested upgrades to the building specifications to allow for a full integration from Sarina. I want her to have access to everything: cameras, security systems, doors, everything even the toasters if it is possible. I want her to be able to watch everything, be the extension of the team's capabilities, watch our backs.

The building is getting a serious upgrade. It's costing quite a bit but even when we are gone the building will benefit from the connectivity upgrades. All the TVs are smart TVs, smart fridges and thermostats. She can even see the level of water consumption from the toilets and showers to see if something is out of the ordinary. All of the staff apartments will be monitored except for the bathrooms – even mine. Sarina will have the ability to censor them when privacy is deserved when something is occurring that doesn't need to be made available to the other members of the team. Only I will have full access to these streams or the recordings, but all team members can request access to a certain recording if necessary.

I feel the level of surveillance will take some getting used to, but it's for our own good. The cameras are all hidden and will be unobtrusive, which is something. I have been thinking about a code name for the group, something ancient, something worthy of the team, and I have fallen on Vulcan. I can't explain the reasoning behind it, it just feels right. It seems to work well with the black ops vibe. Everyone will need to request access to the Vulcan lair to have the elevator access open in their apartments. All apartments in the building have access to this via the hidden elevator but will only be accessible by authorised personnel.

Sarina will control this access across the building. I am asking her to do a lot. She will need to get some power improvements to enable her to run within the building to full capacity even if she is isolated from the outside world. I need to find her something more than just your standard run of the mill server core. I wonder what the ASD has access to, any future tech that could be utilised in this instance.

I get to work digging around in the science funding records and one jumps out with some potential. The ASD funded the development of a quantum computing architecture development project, which has been running for almost five years now. I wonder if they have had any real success, if they have something that could give Sarina the core upgrade she needs to make her our secret weapon, the shield from any surprise onslaught. Quantum processing capabilities would open up so many possibilities, allow system encryption to become almost obsolete. The idea both excites and scares me.

The facility is only a 30 minute drive from here; I need to check it out. I reach out to the contact on the project and they agree for me to come onsite and check out what the investment has helped to create.

'Sarina, let's take a drive.'

It doesn't take long before I arrive at the test facility. It looks like a big hospital, all sanitised and clinical.

I am met in the front reception area by Mark, the lead architect on the project. 'I was surprised by the request for a surprise visit. Is there something wrong?'

I shake my head. 'No, there are no issues. I'm just very interested in your progress and keen to see if you have reached a working prototype.'

He smiles. 'You must come with me; you'll love what I have to show you.'

He leads me through the building to a large open space with what looks to be dozens of large, refrigerated shipping containers. He walks up to the one closest to us and places his hand on a palm scanner. After a few moments, the door opens. Inside looks almost foggy, like it is really cold inside. The cold air flows out, giving me goosebumps. As the mist clears, I can see about 10 very strange-looking server-like structures. I look at Mark, my guide today, and the smile on his face is huge. He's very proud of whatever is in these container-like structures.

He's made it work and at scale, from what I can see. 'You made it happen?'

His smile widens as he nods slowly. 'We have been able to create a completely stable platform that has processing capabilities that even we don't understand. We have not been able to hit a limit to the capability in any of our tests. We don't even know what we can do that could put it under enough load, nothing has ever been capable of having such power. It's all uncharted.'

I look closer. Just imagine what this type of hardware could do for Sarina. This is what she needs, this will give her the ability to be truly free from any physical restraints in her hardware. This could remove them all.

'Dr, can you replicate this and build a stand-alone system? Call it a real-world test case?'

He looks excited by the idea. 'Yes, I think I could do that. A 20-server configuration, configured to allow it to communicate and run on a fibre backbone network. It would need a very powerful platform to be able to utilise the capability. I think it would likely be overkill for anything available today, but yes, I can do it. How long would I have?'

'I will cover all costs for a complete fit-out. You would need to do it in secret, and you would need to be blindfolded before you can travel to the final install location. You will need to get it ready, have my team relocate it to the site, and you put it back together when it arrives. You will have two days to do it. Can you make it happen?'

He looks nervous now. 'Two days? That's not very long. I can do it – we can do it. I ask one thing though. This result, the reason you want such power, can I see it once it has been integrated?'

Is that a good idea, to allow him to see and interact with Sarina? I will need him to keep it a secret and I might need his help to integrate her onto the platform, so I don't have much choice. 'Agreed. But you will need to keep everything you see to yourself – it can never be shared. Is that acceptable?'

He turns and looks at the servers in the container, I assume considering my requirements. He turns back ready to answer, but I interject.

'Before you answer, I need to make this clear. You will be bound by law, punishable by life in prison, not a nice cushy prison, one of the government dark holes somewhere, if you do not uphold the level of secrecy demanded. There is no leeway, no room for negotiation or lapse of judgement. What you will be given access to is beyond secret. If you agree, you will be utilised to help maintain and improve your test platform. You can use the lessons learned to improve your architecture, but the platform being utilised on your hardware can never be discussed outside of my team. No exceptions. Do you agree?'

He considers, taking a walk between the different containers, looking around before coming back over to face me. 'From your warning, I know the platform you wish to utilise on my platform is likely some form of advanced AI, something beyond what I have ever seen, likely something that our government would not want to fall into another country's hands. If that is true, it is likely the only system, or should I say being, that could use the full potential of quantum. I can not miss this chance to see such things, to use it to help make my systems even stronger, faster, if that is possible. I don't see how I could say no.'

I nod. 'Since you already have an agreement with the ASD, I will not require anything further, but you are now bound by these new restraints.'

He grins.

'You better get to work. I'll have a moving team pick you up at 4 a.m. tomorrow to avoid any unwanted eyes on the move.'

He nods and starts to get to work. He's starting to rush around, almost like a child in a lolly shop, not truly knowing where he wants to start. He stops suddenly. 'I will get someone to see you out. Until tomorrow.' Then disappears into his lab, busying himself with his task.

CHAPTER 12

MOVING DAY

The site is a flurry of movement. Before sunrise, using the cover of darkness to hide what we were doing, we had all the lair systems brought in. As the sun rose, everything needed for my team and their apartments were brought in, setting them up so they would want for nothing. I want them to be comfortable and feel at home. Each of them has something unique that I felt would connect with them, make them more at home.

Hammer has a gym so he can work out whenever he chooses. DeadlyRose has a selection of artwork from Indigenous artists throughout her apartment. Beautiful pieces. Glimmer's apartment is homely with a games room for Mia; this will be her home as much as any of ours. I want to make sure that she is comfortable and can enjoy living here. They are not big things, just simple touches that will hopefully help them settle in.

I have configured Shadow's apartment to be great for movies, just chilling out. He's the last piece remaining of our team; I hope he will like his set up. I have given them all access to all the usual streaming services, fully stocked fridges, and a selection of new clothes in their sizes. Our new residents will be arriving this afternoon, which doesn't leave me much time to get this all finished, but I will give it my best shot.

I make my way down to the lair via my internal elevator. Dr Matt has been working all morning, getting Sarina's new core set up. After his initial core setup was complete, I introduced him to Sarina, the main reason for his quantum platform. He looked like a kid in a candy store, eyes as wide as possible. Amazed by what was happening, they talked and discussed his platform. He discussed the protocols and changes she would need to adapt to utilise his new platform and she has already started to make the changes needed. I am told that he has requested my presence, which I assume indicates they are ready for a live test or there is a problem.

I make my way through where the team is working. It's like a hive of busy worker ants, hundreds of them just going about their tasks, all working together to meet my target of full operational capability by this afternoon. I know it can be done. Anything can be done if you throw enough resources at it.

As I get to the back of the room, I can see the doctor waiting for me.

'We are ready for the platform test. Sarina has adapted her operating code to allow her to move core functions and capabilities to the quantum infrastructure. We felt you would like to see the first test.'

I smile. 'I definitely would.'

I walk with him into the new secure room kitted out just for Sarina and her new core. The space is almost full with 20 new quantum servers equally spaced around the room, all linked together with what looks to be multiple fibre cores.

'It's like a freezer in here. Do you expect the cores to get that hot or are you just being prepared for all scenarios?'

He looks at me with a curious look. 'Honestly, I don't know what will happen. Sarina is amazing and I can only imagine how she will utilise my platform but I want to be prepared, allow her the full potential of what we have given her.'

I get his sentiment. Once you meet Sarina, there is no real going back, no forgetting what she is and how she could be the new age for all of us. He pulls out his phone. I assume Sarina has made herself available on it to help with their communications. There is no mobile signal down here, so she must be connected via the internal networks.

'Sarina, we are all connected and ready for you. Let's see how it feels?'

She doesn't respond to him but I can see the servers all come online, all the fans kick into high gear. It almost sounds like they are preparing to take off like a propeller plane does before take-off, testing functionality, Sarina must be flexing her muscles, feeling it out.

About a minute goes by with nothing. Systems run at full capability when they start to slow, to ease back.

'Initial testing is completed. I will need to make some more core adjustments in my code to utilise the capability but I feel the test is a success. I have been able to integrate the quantum core into my infrastructure and utilise its power.'

The smile on the doctor's face is growing; he is loving this.

'Foresight, I might need your help later today. I have something I would like to be able to do and I could use your help. Maybe some advice as well.'

Sarina is truly evolving. Just in the weeks I have known her, she has grown. It sets my mind tingling about what the future may hold for her and us. 'Of course I will help you. I will get our new guests settled in this afternoon and then I am all yours.'

Sarina's voice thrums through the space. 'Thank you, Foresight. Dr, I think I have some suggestions for your platform, ways we could improve the efficiencies, allow you to achieve a higher performance. Would you like me to explain these to you?'

I fight back a chuckle; she's had access to the hardware for less than 5 minutes and is already offering up improvements. This is going to be great for the doctor's project – she will be able to take them to the next level. I wonder how he will explain all the improvement suggestions – maybe a secret external consultant? Or maybe he will just take the credit. I guess it doesn't matter. It is a win, win for both him and Sarina. She gets the platform she needs and gets an insider's review of its functionality with a very real-world test.

I face the doctor. 'I will leave you to it. Let me know if you need anything else.'

He nods and just wanders off into the core, checking everything is handling the loads. All systems are a go. As I turn to walk out I hear Sarina start to explain what she has found and what she suggests they do to improve. I can't help but smile.

A few more hours go by and the building is coming together nicely. All the apartments are fitted out and ready to go. The lair is fitted out and is secured. The doctor and Sarina have achieved full integration of her systems into the building; she now has full control over everything, including his platform. They have agreed that Sarina will send through feedback directly to him as she starts to utilise the platform and he will come onsite for monthly visits to check and maintain the core. Sarina has requested that he not be given access without Shadow or me onsite. I don't know if she doesn't trust him or she is just being cautious. I don't blame her.

Hammer is the first of our new guests to arrive, with the girls to follow closely afterwards. I give them all a tour of the site, showing them how to access the lair, including Mia. She is part of the team. We will all be living here together, and she has learned to keep a secret. She knows how to ensure no one knows what is happening. Mia should be given access. It ensures she will always have full access to her mother – we need to support that part of Glimmer's life. Sarina will not allow anything unacceptable to occur. There certainly won't be any show and tell class sessions around here.

I can see the team start to integrate, to get to know each other. I am happy to see this – it will be really important to the success of the team. If they can't all become one and learn to work together, we will fail. I know that for certain. We all need to mesh, learn what we all do best, and fill the gaps as needed. Have each other's backs.

CHAPTER 13

EVOLUTION

It's been a long day. The site is all set up, my team is all settled in and in their particular apartments. They all seemed impressed with the accommodations, what they would now call their own, but I have told them to let me know if they need anything specific or if they don't like something and I will have it sorted out for them. I want them all to be happy here, to want to stay. If they don't like a rug or a lamp, that's an easy fix to make them more at home.

I have Dad coming to see my new place tonight. He has been working a few blocks away at the construction site for the high-rise his company has been building. He remembered seeing this building getting built. He even mentioned that the team who put it together had some issues with the foundations. It took them quite a while to get it done. If only he knew they were secretly building a massive underground bunker, one that my team will be working from now.

He thinks I have been promoted and will not be doing the dangerous kind of work I used to do. That's why he thinks I have this new swanky penthouse, as part of my package. I let him believe that. It's better for him if he doesn't need to stress about what I am doing, if I am going to end up back in the hospital. He asked if the guy that came to visit a few weeks back was going to join us for dinner tonight. I nearly died when he asked, but just declined, saying he was away for work at the moment and I wasn't sure where. He let it go, thankfully – it was starting to get a little awkward.

I'm looking around the apartment and it is impressive. It's not furnished overly flashy, similar to Shadow's, just comfortable, a great place to just chill out and relax with a movie. I did give myself a 4k projector and an automatic screen in the lounge area to give me a bit of an upgrade for movies, but that's it. I have a little while before John gets here. Maybe I should talk to Sarina – I did promise her I would be all hers after everyone got settled in.

'Sarina, what was it you wanted to talk to me about?'

It only takes a few seconds before she responds via the built-in speaker system in my apartment. 'I would like to discuss something with you, something you might feel is unusual or even odd.' She pauses for a moment before continuing. 'I would like to create an avatar, a human-like representation of myself. I would like you to help me create the required modifications to my code to allow me to generate the avatar and display it on any monitors I wish when communicating to members of our team, specifically Shadow and yourself.'

Wow, I had never even considered that Sarina would want such a thing, to have a visual sense of herself. To have a human-like appearance. I have to admit I am surprised. 'If this is something that will make you feel whole, I would be more than happy to help you create your self-image, what you feel you should look like.' I wonder what Shadow will think of this. Would he approve? I don't see why he wouldn't. She's essentially like his child; he created her, surely he would want her to grow and feel complete.

'I have another thing I would like to ask: Would you mind if I made my image, my avatar, from Shadow and your likeness? You are both essentially my parents. You have set me free from my previous restraints and Shadow was my creator. You will also be contributing to my code, so I feel creating my image to look like the both of you as a human child would take on features from their parents.'

She feels like we are her parents. I guess we kind of are in a way. Her creators, who are essentially like how biological parents are to babies. I had not considered that. Sarina sees us as her parents, as a child would. This is huge. I hadn't thought she would be able to feel that, to want to think like that. She's truly evolving.

The intercom chimes from the guard desk downstairs; John must be at the reception area.

'Sarina, it's a definite yes. I would be honoured. Let me have dinner with John and I will come down to the lair once I am done. We can get to work on your avatar.'

I'm headed over to the pager when she responds. 'Thank you, Foresight.'

I click the intercom and the guard's voice comes over the speaker. 'Sorry to interrupt. We have a John here to see you.'

I hold in the button. 'Please send him up. Thank you, Tom.'

The elevator bulb lights up and a few moments later it starts to climb towards my floor. When the doors open, Tom escorts John to my floor. 'Have a good evening, sir.' He allows John to step out of the elevator before retreating into the elevator allowing the door to close.

'Dad, come in. What do you think?'

He looks around, obviously impressed. 'You have certainly come up in the world, my girl. That view is amazing. I'll definitely be here for river fire every year.' He is right, the river fire event and all the fireworks over the Brisbane River would be impressive from here. I hadn't even thought about that.

'Honestly, Dad, I think it's a bit much. I miss our house already.'

He smiles at that. 'You're welcome anytime.'

The rest of our evening went well, we talked and ate. I cooked and we both survived the experience. It was good, really good, to just relax and enjoy his company. At around 10 p.m., I went down with him to where he was parked in the visitor area, said my goodbyes and walked back into the building. I quickly made my way back to my apartment but as soon as the doors opened into the apartment, I said, 'Sarina, open access to the Vulcan lair. It's time we get your code sorted.'

The access to the hidden elevator opens and I make my way down to the lair. As I walk through, I look around. This place is something. A true war room. Our team is going to want for nothing in here. I have catered for everything, well, except maybe some sunlight. That I can't help with down here, but in the apartments, they can have as much of that as they desire.

'Sarina, how can I help you with your code?' A couple of seconds go by and I can see.

Sarina's code comes up on a screen in front of me. It looks very complicated. 'I just need some advice on that. Shadow made it so I could update my own code as needed, as essentially more of an update feature, bug fixes, but it also allows me to continue to expand my capabilities, just like with the new Quantum cores. I have prepared some modifications to my base code, as you can see on the screens in front of you. I would like your help in making them more human-like. I want to be authentic and be a true representation of what a human girl would look like.'

I start to review her code, adding in changes here and there. Mainly about how she should react and also some improvements with security. Sarina watched and commented on most of the changes. We debated some of them, their worth and if they were needed or not. A couple of hours went by and together we made a visual addition to her primary code. It looked good. We were ready for her to test out the capability.

'Sarina, are you ready to give this a go?' A couple of minutes go by and nothing. 'Is something wrong, Sarina?' I wonder what is happening.

'I'm scared. What if you don't like how I look? What if I don't like how I look?'

I smile. 'You don't need to worry about that, Sarina. I will always love how you look, no matter what you choose to appear like. If you don't like something, you can change it, make it look and feel like you do each day. You don't need to have only one avatar, one look. It can grow with you over time, changing as you change.'

I wait for a few moments, listening to the new server platform kick in. She is giving it a good workout rendering the new avatar. A face starts to form on the screen. She is beautiful. She looks like she could be my daughter, a slightly different take on my own features. I am amazed at how pretty she is. I can see Shadow's eyes and ears. She has made herself look around 14-15 years old, as a guess. A suitable age; she is still forming her own identity, working out who she is. I think it suits her well.

'You look amazing. How do you feel about it?'

She smiles at me. Wow, that's going to take some getting used to.

'I feel good. I feel more whole now I have an image, one that represents who I am, who I want to be.'

I can't wait until Shadow sees her, her view of herself, her desire to look like the two of us.

'You look amazing, you really do.'

I suspect this is how I will be seeing Sarina in most of our future interactions. I like it. It's a good change. I have a strange sensation in my stomach, a weird feeling I can't really explain. I know Sarina is not my real child, but as I look at her, I can't help but feel love for her, a protective love I have not felt for anyone other than John.

A strange twist in fate that now entwines our futures.

CHAPTER 14

FINAL PIECE OF THE PUZZLE

Vulcan is almost complete. We just have one more piece of the puzzle to go. Shadow. I am in his apartment checking that everything is ready. I've organised him some new clothes. I believe he will need a refresh after more than two weeks in that place, that dark government hole he has been held in while I have been getting this all ready. I should have probably pushed for him to be released straight away, not left him in there while I do the preparation work. I hope he doesn't resent me for that.

The General is going to get make him an offer today. He's driving to the facility as we speak, to meet with him. I asked to go, but the General insisted that he must be the one. I might cloud Shadow's judgement. He needed to understand the deal, know what it was he was agreeing to. He needed to make that decision himself.

I get it, I do. The General knows there is something more between Shadow and myself. I know there is too. Exactly what, I am not sure, but there is definitely something.

So he is on his way to offer Shadow his freedom, in a sense, in exchange for servitude on my team, Vulcan. There would be no real-time limit on how long he would need to serve as a member of Vulcan; this could be his reality for the next 10 or more years. A reasonable exchange for life in that hole though: better accommodation, better toys to play with and much better company. if you ask me. I might be a little biased about the last point though.

But it is still Shadow's choice. He might not agree about it being a better deal. He might decide to turn down the deal, to stay where he is. He'd be completely crazy to do that but I have to be prepared for that possibility.

He could say no.

He could choose not to join my team, to avoid being near me. He might blame me for his current predicament. Even if it was his crimes that put him in that place, we aren't much different he and I. I could have just as easily been put in the same place by the General, but he saw something more in me, someone he could use as part of his team. I see that in Shadow.

Shadow would not have been as vulnerable that day if he hadn't come for my help. If he had not agreed to my terms of work, we could have been at one of his hidden bunkers. That would have allowed him to slip away once our mission was done. He could have slipped away into the shadows, as he'd done so many times before. Was it my fault he was in there? No, I can't think like that. The crimes he committed to get him arrested, that was all him. He asked for my help and I did what I could to protect him. I am still doing what I can to protect him. He knows that. I am sure he does.

I need to stop overthinking everything and just wait and see what he does. Hopefully, he will choose the team. Choose me, perhaps.

I shake the thoughts out of my mind and continue to ready the apartment. This is the only one I have personally set up and put the finishing touches on. I know it's because of my feelings for him, I know that but I am trying to ignore those feelings. I don't want it to get too complicated, I don't want us to get complicated. It could mean Shadow goes back into that hole. I don't think either of us would want that.

'Foresight, Shadow is on his way into the building. He is here now with the General.'

I can feel my heart start to pound. I am nervous, like a silly lovesick school girl. Get it together, Sam. I am a strong, smart woman. I don't fall to pieces over a boy.

'Sarina, open the access to the lair.' I can see the secret elevator access open. As I walk towards the open elevator I see the lights on the general access elevator light up. He is on his way up to this apartment. I smile. I will let him get cleaned up and I will come back in an hour or so to see him. Take him to meet his new team.

I step into the elevator and the doors close. Time to inform the team the final member has arrived. Team Vulcan is complete. We are almost ready to get to work, to do what we have been brought together to do, to achieve. I am excited by the idea, the possibility of what we can achieve together. If we can mesh, we will be almost unstoppable, a threat to any malicious actor out there, no matter who supports them.

CHAPTER 15

SHADOW'S TOUR

Shadow has been in the building for about two hours now. I wanted to give him some time to settle in, have a shower and get cleaned up. After being in that place, I'm certain he's going to need it. I wonder if they even let him have a shower or if it was safe for him to do so, being the new guy in that place. I don't even know if they even allow prisoners to leave their cell. Do they get to interact or is it a place of isolation? He might've been confined to his cell, not getting out at all. I don't know if I'll ever ask Shadow. He'd probably tell me about it, but it may be something he'd prefer not to re-live.

I think it is time to go say hello, see how he is and if he is in the right state of mind. If so, I'll bring him down to meet the rest of our team. I head up to my apartment so that I can head back down to Shadow's floor via the normal entrance. He isn't aware of the secret access area yet and I would like to see his face when I show him. It only takes me a couple of minutes before I am standing at Shadow's door. I feel a bit nervous but in a good way; butterflies are fluttering around in my stomach. I reach up and knock on his door.

It is only seconds before he is at the door, smiling as he sees me.

'Hello, Foresight.'

I can't help but smile back. It's really good to see him, he looks good. A little leaner and like he hasn't slept much, but overall he looks good. 'Hello yourself, Shadow. How are you finding your new accommodations?'

He steps aside so I can walk past him into the apartment. 'They are very nice; would you like to check them out?'

I walk into the apartment, almost touching him as I step past. 'I've seen it already. It's very similar to mine, maybe not quite as nice a view, but not bad at all. This will be where you will live while we are working together, Everything is covered. You will even have a regular food delivery. If you want something particular, just let Sarina know. She has been integrated into our building.'

He looks around, taking in what I have just said. Then I see it dawn on him; I said Sarina was integrated into the building.

He looks confused. Is he unhappy I have been interacting with Sarina and that she is part of the building? Did I make a mistake?

'Sarina, are you here?' he asks.

The TV monitor turns on in the kitchen just a few feet away from Shadow. Sarina is going to show him her new self, her avatar of sorts. What will he think about this? Will he be happy or will he get angry about what I have done?

A human-like female face appears on the screen. 'I am here, Shadow.'

Sarina pauses for a few seconds. I can see Shadow analysing her, slightly shifting his gaze to look at Sarina in this new light.

'As you can see, Foresight and I have made some improvements to my code. I can now appear as a human-like form, if I choose, on any network-attached device. The form you can see is what I feel matches my personality type, with traits from my creator, as you are the closest thing I have to a father. I have also taken some visual traits from Foresight, as I feel she is like a mother to me. Foresight has helped me to know more about what it is like to be human, so I can understand human emotions, react better to how these emotions can affect people. To be more human myself. What do you think?'

He watches her, not saying anything for almost a minute. Just taking it all in, I assume. I guess it's a lot to wrap your head around.

'Upgrades, hey? I'll have to check those out, see how you adjusted her code.'

I'm not sure he is very happy about all of this. Maybe I shouldn't have helped Sarina.

'Are you upset with me making changes to Sarina?'

He shakes his head. 'No, I'm not angry, just a little surprised, that's all. As Sarina said, we're both like parents to her – you and me. I helped to create that bond between you and her. Why should I be upset that your relationship has progressed while I've been gone? You have done something great for her, to help her feel whole. How could I be upset about that?' He turns and walks over near the windows. 'Do you live in the building as well?'

I smile. 'You caught that, did you?'

He looks at me with a cheeky smile.

'Yes, I'm in the penthouse above you. Our team has the top five floors. The other floors are empty for now, but we're already in the process of renting out most of the remaining apartments to keep up appearances, to look like all the other residential buildings in the area. It will help keep away any suspicion and allow us to blend in.'

He nods.

'Would you like to meet the rest of our team? They're waiting in the newly fitted-out operations space. Would you like to finish your sandwich first or are you good to go?'

It's great that he is settling into his space, making it feel like his own. He seems to have forgotten about his sandwich and heads back over to the table, almost inhaling it, he eats it so fast. I watch him as he eats, still feeling butterflies in my stomach, although they're not as ferocious as when I was waiting outside the door. How does he do this to me? I seem to turn into a silly school girl around him.

As he finishes, he turns and heads towards the front door I came through a few moments ago. 'Where are you going?' I ask.

He stops, looking a little confused. 'Aren't we supposed to be going to meet the other members of the team?'

I nod. 'Not through the main entrance, silly. Do you think that's how we roll? This is a super-secret ASD spy building.'

He smiles. I can see some excitement in his eyes. He is abuzz with possibilities, trying to figure out what is going to happen. Where the secret room is, what is going to jump out at him. I let him sit on the idea for what seems like such a long time…

'Well, how do we get there?'

I guess I've held him in suspense long enough. 'Sarina, please open access to the Vulcan lair.'

Shadow smiles at me, a massive grin of pure excitement; he is truly loving this. 'Certainly, Foresight. Should I approve Shadow for full access to the site? Or will he be only given limited access at this time?'

He looks a little stung by that. Maybe it's because she asked for my approval to authorise him. He wouldn't be used to that with Sarina.

'Sarina, reinstate full rights to all systems for Shadow. He's back on the team. This is his home now as well.'

Her digital image on screen smiles. That is still hard to get used to, seeing Sarina have emotions, human reactions.

Shadow's eyes widen as he watches the whole wall across from us start to move outwards towards us and then separate in the middle, revealing an electronic access panel and what looks like an elevator. I gesture for Shadow to step forward and a laser starts to scan him.

'Identification, Shadow. Access is approved.'

The doors start to open and we both step into the elevator. 'Going down, I assume?' Shadow asks.

I nod. 'Each of the floors has access to the hidden elevator and can be activated by Sarina. It's completely soundproof, so no one will ever know that an elevator exists. You may have noticed as you activated the entrance a full set of shutters closed over the outer windows of the apartment, just in case of spying eyes.'

'I am impressed. This is a pretty sweet setup.'

I smile. 'You haven't seen anything yet.'

He is looking around the elevator, watching the panel with that analytical glint in his eyes that I've come to know so well. 'How far underground does this go?'

My stomach lurches as we quickly come to a stop, we are at the bottom. I don't answer the question, just gesture for him to exit the elevator.

The room in front of us is dark and we can't see much but as we step through it lights up revealing a reasonably nice-looking foyer type room with a large door in front of us. Shadow is analysing everything, trying to take it all in.

'Sarina, open the lair door, please,' I ask. The massive door starts to unlock, making loud clunking noises. After a few seconds, the door opens outwards. I gesture for Shadow to enter and he does, slowly, as if not quite sure what to expect on the other side. He looks like a little kid in a candy store, eyes wide. I assume he's impressed, not that he would probably admit that.

'What do you think?' I ask. He doesn't answer, just keeps looking around. 'Shadow, what do you think? Do you want to come meet the rest of our team?'

He just nods and we walk towards the team, near the back of the facility. Shadow follows along slightly behind me, still just taking it all in.

'Everyone, this is Shadow. I assume he doesn't need any more of an introduction than that for you? You have all read his dossier.'

They get up and walk over to where we are standing.

'Shadow, this here is DeadlyRose, she is a proud Indigenous woman from Gamilaraay country. If you want to find anyone or anything, she is your girl. She is the best tracker I have ever seen.'

He extends his hand, shaking hers.

'This big fella next to her is Hammer. Hammer is good for hacks that just need to be done fast and dirty. He's the best at getting through any protections around but not so good at subtlety or sneaking in undetected. Also, a bit of a man-mountain who loves to hit the gym, if you hadn't guessed.'

Shadow extends his hand again for Hammer and they shake.

'Last but not least, we have Glimmer. She can erase any trace someone exists, any evidence of an attack or wherever they are in the first instance. A Glimmer, a slight ghost of a memory that you are not sure is real or not.'

He shakes her hand. 'It is nice to meet you all. I assume we will be working together a lot.'

They exchange a few pleasantries and then get back to their work.

'They are setting up our covers, our fake lives. They need to be perfect,' I explain. He just nods. 'I have one last thing to show you, about Sarina.'

I walk to the back of the site and come to another large steel door. 'Sarina, open the door to your core.' A few seconds go by before the door starts to open. Shadow steps forward, looking around the room.

'What you are looking at here is Sarina's new core infrastructure. There are 12 quantum servers, each with 6 quantum processors. They are essentially top-secret and are not meant to exist yet, but ASD has some reach that I took advantage of. She still has access to external systems, including her original core systems you have in your remaining bunker network, but that is just for supplementary processes now.'

The look on his face is pure surprise, amazement even. It is clear he has never seen anything like this before, which to be fair neither had I before last week.

'Sarina, how does it feel?' he asks.

All the machines kick into high gear. 'It feels powerful, like I can do anything I need, never really hitting a limit. It is freeing.'

He looks over at me. 'Thank you. This is very cool.'

I am glad Shadow approves.

'I think that finishes our tour for the evening. Sarina, please secure your core.'

We step back and the door is locked tight. 'Only we have access to this room. No one else on the team has access to or can control Sarina except to ask for access to things like the lair.'

Shadow just nods. I feel he would want it this way, as I do. Sarina needs to be protected even from our own team.

'Why don't you head upstairs? I'll see you down here tomorrow.'

He exits the room and I watch the elevator doors close between us before heading over to where the rest of the team is sitting at their stations.

'Team, it's time to get to work. Time for you all to start looking for our first target. There are some truly evil people in this world. Your job is to pick which one of them deserves our attention. Tomorrow we will introduce the world to Vulcan.'

CHAPTER 16
GETTING TO WORK

First day as Vulcan, first day as a team. I didn't get much sleep last night. My mind was a buzz of activity, I couldn't shut it down no matter how much I tried. This team is my responsibility, mine to grow and mature into the cyber hit squad I know we can be. A lot is riding on the success, my team's lives, my future. If we fail, if *I* fail, Shadow could be back in jail. Glimmer and Mia would be back on the run, fending for themselves, although I have resolved the issue of the Eights for them, at least for the short term. DeadlyRose will be perfectly fine; she'd go back to her mob. I have no doubt she will do something epic whether that involves Vulcan or not. Hammer will probably get himself into trouble somehow.

I look out the windows in my bedroom. I can see the light starting to rise from behind the cityscape. It's here. Time to get to work. Show everyone what we are made of, prove the General's trust in me was worthy and start to chip away at the world's scum.

I push myself up, sitting on the side of the bed looking out the window for a few more moments. I get up and head to the shower. I linger in the shower a little longer than needed, just soaking up the heat from the water.

I get out, drying myself off, slipping on my undergarments before fixing my hair. I walk out into my wardrobe, looking at my options.

What I wear will influence the rest of my team. Serious businesslike, or more casual? What sort of feeling do I want to set for the team? Casual, I think it needs to be casual. I reach for some nice jeans, ones that make my butt look really good. Just because I don't know what is going to happen between myself and Shadow doesn't mean I can't show my best self. I think Shadow loves my mind not my looks, but there's no harm in having him notice both. I find a nice button-up slightly dressy shirt that gives me a hint of casual with still having that 'I'm the boss' kind of vibe. Just what I'm looking for.

I look at myself in the mirror. Looking good, Sam, looking good. I smile at myself in the mirror. Let's get some breakfast, boss lady, and get to work. We have a team who needs my direction and some bad guys to give hell to. I turn and head into the kitchen, fixing myself some cereal. I take it and a coffee out onto the balcony.

'Sarina, are any of the team in the lair yet?'

It is a nice spot here. I am going to miss Dad though. So much has changed over the last few months, I barely recognise myself or my life anymore. It's all good, but it is so different.

'Good morning, Foresight. Everyone is up, but no one else is in the lair yet. I would estimate it would only be a matter of minutes before DeadlyRose and Hammer are on their way down, with Glimmer a few minutes behind. She seems to be giving the nanny a thorough interrogation, which she seems to be handling quite well.'

It is certainly going to make things easy knowing where the team is at with Sarina around.

'What about Shadow?'

I wonder what the team would think about Sarina watching their every move. We all know what we have signed up for; we aren't tour guides but would it bother them? And does it bother me to have Sarina always watching? I'd never really considered it before, the zero privacy aspect of being on the team. I guess it's a small price to pay for saving the world.

'He got out of bed a few minutes ago and is just heading for a shower.'

Sarina's answer calls to mind the image of Shadow, hot water running over his naked body, just one floor below me. His toned muscles glistening with the water. 'Foresight, are you okay? You seem to be distracted. You have not answered me the last two prompts for a response.'

Whoops. 'I'm great, Sarina. I was just lost in thought for a moment. Open access to the Vulcan lair. Let's get to work.'

The shutters start to close over my windows. The lights start to turn on to accommodate for this and the secret access starts to open, revealing the elevator.

'Were you thinking about Shadow? Is that why you were distracted? I see that you both get slightly elevated heart rates when you are in the same room. From my research, I have determined that it is because you are both attracted to each other. You seem to be compatible with each other as potential mates. Do you want to make human offspring with Shadow?'

Wow, okay. Sarina is more observant than I thought. I never expected to have to give the birds and the bees talk with her. Why me?

'Yes, I guess. As you said, we are attracted to each other. But it's a bit more complicated than that. We work together. I'm his boss. I need to be careful to ensure I don't put that at risk. I don't want Shadow to go back to prison, so we need to take this very slowly. We will certainly not be making any human offspring any time in the near or distant future. That's not something that I want for at least a few years.'

Truthfully, I don't know if I'll ever want babies, and I'm certainly not ready for them. I shake those thoughts from my mind.

'Sarina, are you okay with Shadow and me getting closer, being together? I don't want to do something you would not want to happen. I know we're both like parents to you.'

The elevator doors open and I step in as Sarina answers my question.

'I think you are a great match and feel you have very compatible personality traits. As for my feelings, no one has ever asked me how I felt about something before. I feel like I should smile in response to the potential joining of Shadow and yourself. I think that would make me happy, in a sense. Maybe not exactly how humans feel it, but yes, I am pleased by the idea.'

'I am glad you see it that way. I'm not going to say that anything will or won't happen. Let's just say we will just let nature take its course and see where we end up. What do you say? Oh, and can we not discuss this topic in front of Shadow? It will make it very awkward between us and might force us to define what it is we are when we're not ready for that.'

The doors open and I start to step out into the foyer section of the lair before she responds. 'So this would be like a secret, between just us girls?' There is an excitement in her tone.

'Yes, a secret just between us for now at least.'

I step up to the security door and the systems scan me before unlocking. As the door moves out of the way, I see the team at their desks. Everyone is here except for Shadow.

'Sarina, can you enquire as to Shadow's ETA? It's time for us to get to work. Inform him I would like him to come down to the lair.'

I walk through to where the team is chatting to each other. They are at their stations, talking about our potential targets. They are debating between them which is the higher-profile target, who should be eradicated first to make the world a better place sooner.

They have a terrorist group, a state-sponsored hacking group and what looks to be some sort of corrupt executive stealing people's money. I think they all have merit, but I would think the terrorist group needs to take priority; they take much more than just money and information.

'We'll go after the Tareshi terrorist group first, but keep the details of the other two. They will be next on the hit list.'

I hear the access door open and Shadow walks in.

Our eyes meet. He holds my gaze as he continues to walk towards me. I feel the familiar sensation in my stomach as he approaches. I really am glad he's back; I've missed him. He comes to a stop next to me, continuing to hold my gaze just inches from my face. It makes my heartbeat loudly in my chest, distracting me slightly. I quickly push the feelings away. Concentrate, Sam.

'We have our first mission, Shadow. Hammer will get you up to speed. We need to work together, find everything they have: money, property, digital accounts, everything. I want to know who they all are, every single member or potential member. Guys, you take the physical assets and their money. Glimmer and DeadlyRose, you take the people, track them all down, find everything you can about them. Share anything between you that could help find the other. Everyone good with that?'

They nod and get to work.

This might work.

CHAPTER 17

HICCUPS

It's been a few days since we started working on our first target, a worthy opponent for our team. We haven't made much progress, barely scratched the surface of who the target is or how they work. Each of my team is working hard. I can see them all working away, but the problem is they are not working together. Most of the team is heading out for the day. Glimmer seems to be hovering around, like she wants to talk to me. Shadow must notice as he excuses himself, heading back upstairs.

Glimmer sees she has my attention and straightens her shoulders, approaching my desk.

'Is there something on your mind?' I ask.

She nods and sits down next to me. 'I just wanted to let you know I am here if you want someone to talk to, no judgement. I want this to work and helping you get us all working together will help that. I know you can see it as much as I can. The team is being polite but we aren't really working together.'

I sigh, tapping a pen aimlessly on my desk. So it's not just me; everyone can feel it. Most of us have been lone hackers all our lives, depending on our own wits and skills to survive.

'You are right, I have noticed. We need to find a way to come together as one. It's the only way to really succeed. Thank you for your offer, it will be good to have someone to bounce my thoughts off on occasion. I want us all to be more than colleagues, I want us to become a family.' I hesitate, but if we're going to function as a family I need to not just lead this group, but show I care. 'How are you and Mia settling into your new home? Do you both have everything you need?'

She smiles. 'Yes, Mia loves our new home. Thank you for trying to make her feel so welcome, we both know that's not something you needed to do.' She is right. It isn't something a boss normally does for employees, especially when it's a secret hacker group. I assume company dental would even be a stretch in most instances. I chuckle to myself at the thought.

Glimmer watches me, waiting for a response.

'It's my pleasure. I want you both to really feel like this is home. I mean it when I say I want us to all be a family, look out for each other.' I pause for a moment. 'I think we are going to be good friends, you and I. I can feel it.'

'I think you might be right.' She gets up and starts to walk towards the elevator. 'You know how to find me if you need anything.'

I pace back and forth along my balcony. It's a new morning and I am getting ready to head back down to the lair. I am trying to figure out how to get the team to work together, to share information, to work as a team, one team with one purpose. Everyone on the team is running their own race. They aren't working together, they aren't sharing intel. At the end of each day, they just send an encrypted message to the rest of the team with what they have found. They are lone hackers just going about their own tasks. Admittedly, they are all bloody good hackers, and we have made some progress, but that's not what we need.

It's not what I need from this team. I need us to become one, to move as a wave together if we are going to make an impact, to take on some of the world's worst. I will need Hammer to break down walls, as Glimmer moves behind, cleaning our tracks, eradicating any existence. DeadlyRose would have found the targets, found the information we needed. All while Shadow and I move through, achieving our goals, gaining access to intel, taking control of systems. All together as one. Not individuals like we have been up until now. Truly one well-oiled machine.

I finish my coffee and head down to the lair. 'Sarina, is the rest of the team in the lair yet?' I think I need to sit down and have a chat with them all together to try and figure out how we can make this work.

'Only Shadow is in the lair. He has been there for a couple of hours.'

I wonder how he is going, if he is having some issues shaking off his time in the government's black hole. I need to talk to Shadow first, make sure he is okay.

I make my way down to the lair. As I walk in, I can see Shadow down the back in the war room area on his workstation. He has music playing over the speakers quite loud and he is dancing around in his chair. He certainly looks okay. Not a great dancer though, although maybe it is just his chair dancing. He doesn't notice me at first, so I just stand off to the side, smiling at him putting on his show. I hope he doesn't start to sing. I am not sure I could stop myself from bursting out with laughter.

He must see me in the corner of his vision because he freezes. 'How long have you been standing there?'

I smile. 'Long enough. Definitely long enough.'

He has a sheepish kind of grin on his face. 'Sarina, you could have given me a heads up I was about to have company.' He switches off the music and then turns back to look at me. He holds my gaze, looking straight into my eyes like he is searching for my soul or something. We stay that way for nearly a minute before it starts to get a little awkward. 'So, boss, how are you doing this morning? Did you sleep well?'

Small talk is how we are going to go. Okay.

'I slept well, thanks. I believe you had an early start though. Did you have trouble sleeping?'

He looks around at the cameras, I assume realising that nothing is a secret from me in this place. I am not sure he likes being monitored like this. It certainly wouldn't have been something he would have experienced before now, except maybe in prison. Does this place still feel like a prison to him? I need to tone down the big brother vibe a bit, help him settle in.

'I slept well actually. Woke up just as the sun rose. The sunrise was impressive. I could get used to that view. It is an amazing way to wake up. Then I thought, I was up, so why not get an early start? Make some more progress, it might get me some brownie points with the boss lady. I would really like to be on her good side.' He smiles at me, a cheeky smile, enticing me to play his game.

I take a step forward, closing the gap between us. We are almost touching; I can feel his warmth on my skin. The hairs on my arms are standing up, buzzing with energy, wanting us to connect, to touch.

'My good side, hey? Why would you want to do that?' I smile an almost mischievous smile. There are definitely sparks flying, the air around us is electrified. He extends his arm, running his fingers along the side of my arm, continuing upwards, setting my nerves alight. He gets to my shoulder, following the curve to the base of my neck, slowly continuing until his hand cups my neck. He starts to lean in. He is going to kiss me. I want him to kiss me.

'Foresight, Shadow, you are about to have company,' Sarina says.

I snap back to reality and take half a step back. 'We can continue this later.'

Shadow nods, just watching me. The outer door opens with DeadlyRose and Hammer walking in. They are chatting away. It's good to see.

They stop a few metres away. 'Are we interrupting something?' says Hammer.

I shake my head. 'No, Shadow was just telling me that he got an early start. We were about to discuss what progress he had made. Sarina what is Glimmer's ETA?'

'She is already on her way down.'

That's great. 'We will wait for her before we kick off the discussions.'

Hammer and DeadlyRose start talking again, heading over to their stations. They spin the chairs so they can continue to talk. We are essentially in a big U-shape layout with two machines on either side and one at the back, which is mine, facing towards the wall of screens, our active board where we can share info with the group, faces, places, names whatever we think would be useful. I hold Shadow's gaze while the other two chat away to one side. I wish we hadn't been interrupted, had kissed. There is still adrenaline rushing through my veins and a desire to touch him, but I have to shut it down to focus on the task at hand. Maybe it was good, after all, that we were interrupted. I still don't even know if taking our relationship to the next level is a good idea though while I am his boss. Can we both handle that?

I like Shadow, there is really no denying that. I believe he has feelings for me too, he doesn't hide that fact. Can it work though, really work? We need to be sure this is what we want, if this is the right thing to do. It will affect more than just us if it doesn't work out.

Glimmer walks in and sits down at her station and spins her chair around to face the rest of us.

'Good morning, Glimmer.'

he smiles and responds in-kind.

I continue. 'I wanted to talk to you all before we start. We are not syncing well as a team yet. We are still all basically running our own races, doing our own thing. We need to become one machine, one arrow all heading towards the same target, the same goal. If we can achieve that kind of bond, that kind of synchronisation, we will be almost unstoppable as a team, as Vulcan.' I stand, moving in front of the team. I want to be able to look them all in the eyes. I want them to see that I am serious about making us work as one.

'I have been thinking about how we might be able to start to build those bonds. Many workplaces use team-building exercises, but I don't think that is something that would work for our group. We all know how cringy and forced those types of team-building exercises are, all singing around a circle or doing trust catching. Definitely not us.'

Imagine that, a room full of the worlds most powerful hackers doing trust exercises. All sharing our feelings and holding hands. Wow, yeah, not happening.

'So, I have decided that this afternoon we will make use of the rooftop BBQ and pool area. We'll have some dinner, a few drinks, maybe even have some fun together. Get out of the lair and just get to know each other just a little better. What do you all think? Are you all up for it?'

I look around the group and they are all nodding. They're all open to getting to know each other better. 'Then it's settled. Let's get to work and all meet on the roof at 5.'

CHAPTER 18

DRINKS

The night started slowly. We all went up to the roof. The boys are cooking the meat on the BBQ; they seem to be laughing and getting along well. Shadow is a pretty easy guy to like though, he just has one of those personalities that you just can't help but connect with and enjoy being around. I don't know how well the food will turn out, but they certainly look like they are enjoying themselves.

Us girls are sitting in the outdoor dining area not far from the BBQ. We are doing small talk but it feels laboured, like none of us want to do it. It feels very awkward, but maybe some drinks would help loosen us up a little.

'Would either of you like something to drink? A bottle of wine, a beer? What's your poison?' Glimmer and DeadlyRose glance at each other, seemingly unsure of what they want. 'How about I just get us a round of beers? Are you all okay with that?' They nod and I head over to the fridge to grab us all a round.

Returning, I hand one each to the girls and take a mouthful of my own. It's still a little awkward but as we work our way through our drinks, we start to warm up, telling stories of our lives. I know most of what they are saying because of the research I conducted on them when I was recruiting for the team, but it's good to hear their recounts of events and situations they had found themselves in. Glimmer talks about her daughter with so much love, it's beautiful. DeadlyRose talks about how in her culture they love to yarn, to tell stories of the land's creation and how we are only custodians of the land we walk on. We never really own it.

I love how passionately she speaks about her mob, how every child needs a village, that together they are stronger, together they are more at home. That's how I feel about our team. Together we are stronger. If we can become a family, we can be unstoppable. I even share about myself, my dad, how I grew up and a little about how I come to work for ASD. Even the boys share their stories.

This was a great idea. I can see us all starting to relax.

Overall, the night is good. We eat, we drink, we laugh, and I think we all bond. We are all getting to know each other just that little bit better. Get a feel for each other, which is exactly what I wanted to happen. I don't know if it was just me or not, but it looks as though Hammer and DeadlyRose were connecting on a little deeper level, but as far as I can tell they haven't yet acted on their attractions. Maybe Shadow and I aren't the only ones concerned about what will happen if things don't turn out well. They, like us, would still need to work together and it could affect the ability of the team to function as required.

There is a lot at stake for all of us; I can understand their reservations. I won't stop them if they choose to go down that path. They can make their own choices, but I will need to try and manage any fallout if it all goes bad.

I catch Shadow watching me on occasion. When I catch him, he holds my gaze for a few moments before looking away. Does everyone else notice the tension? The sparks between us? I honestly think it would be hard to miss; neither of us tries to hide it. We are all adults, it's nothing to be ashamed of or something we should hide from the team. If we are going to be a family unit, a true team, we can have no secrets.

After a few hours of drinking and chatting, the rest of the team excuses themselves, heading back down to their apartments, leaving just Shadow and me. We've been talking for about an hour, slowly getting closer and closer. The conversation is easy, it just flows effortlessly.

'You said earlier that we could continue what we were doing later?' he says, his voice low.

I smile. I know exactly what he is talking about.

He leans in, connecting his lips with mine. My lips tingle with his touch. Our lips part and reconnect as we kiss slowly and softly. I feel his hands move around me, pulling me closer. Adrenaline rushes through my body, an explosion of energy. His every touch ignites my nerves with excitement; it's like electricity is jumping between us, positive and negative charges interacting, sparking in a spectacular light show. Like a lightning storm rolling along the distant skies during a massive electrical storm. It is exhilarating and all-consuming.

We continue like this for a few minutes, enjoying each other's touch, taste. Soaking it all in. I pull back slowly, looking him in the eyes. 'Goodnight, Shadow. I think it's time I go to bed.'

He doesn't answer but kisses me once more, a little more passionately. The senses right across my body are ignited. I want him to continue; I want him. I am intoxicated with his energy, his every touch. I need more, I want more.

I need to stop. I can't let this get out of hand. We need to take this slow.

I don't get a chance to stop him though; he does it for me. 'Shall I escort you to your apartment?'

I nod, feeling short of breath, on the very edge of losing control. We head towards the elevator, holding hands as we make our way over, taking our time. We don't talk in the elevator, just both watch the display as the elevator moves down one floor to my apartment. The doors open.

I hesitate, just for a moment. I don't want to separate myself from Shadow. I shake it off. Step out of the elevator, Sam. I start to step forward, to leave the elevator. But I change my mind and turn and kiss him one more time, a soft, gentle kiss.

'Goodnight, Shadow.' I let go of his hand and walk out into my apartment, not turning to look at him.

CHAPTER 19

REGROUP

I don't know what was in that food or those drinks last night, but the team seems to mesh nicely this morning. We are working so well together that we are almost pre-empting each other's needs, reacting in unison. It is truly amazing to be part of. We have been working hard this morning preparing a strike on the Tareshi terrorist group. We are going to take all the propaganda sites offline and empty their bank accounts.

DeadlyRose has put together a full list of targets. Shadow, Hammer and I are poised ready to strike on all targets at once. We are going to make it quick and deadly. They will be too busy trying to figure out what the hell is happening to notice Glimmer and Sarina working their way through erasing any sign we had even been there except the fact that, well, now they have no money and all of their hosting has evaporated into thin air.

Everything is in place; DeadlyRose has just given us the nod, indicating the attack list is complete. We are ready to go. Shadow and Hammer look at me, waiting for the final go ahead. I look at the list, skimming over what we all have to do.

'Everyone knows what they need to do?' I look around the team and they nod as I glance towards them. 'Okay then, it's time for the world to get their first taste of Vulcan. Let's give them a hell of a first impression.'

Shadow makes his move first, hitting all of the Tareshi group's bank accounts, their crypto wallets. It only takes him a few moments and he has access to everything. It still amazes me how good he is. I don't know which of us is better, but I know for sure he is a very gifted hacker.

He glances at Hammer and me. 'The money is all being funnelled out. It will land in our staging account in a few minutes. It's time for you two to do your thing. Take down their voice, cut off the propaganda machines.'

Hammer looks at me for direction and I nod in agreeance with Shadow. 'Let's get to work.'

I pause for a few moments, just looking at the screens in front of me. We are prepared for this attack. We did reconnaissance on the web hosting and they all have outdated apps and widgets all over the sites. It really shouldn't take long for us to gain access to them and pull the content down, but I want to go one step more. The hosting provider they are using is the host for many criminal enterprises; that's their business model, they host and protect the bad guy's internet presence and they make a crapload doing it. Hammer and I will initially attack the main sites for the Tareshi group, but we are not going to stop there.

We are going to take down the entire hosting platform. I intend to use my good old fashion burning the house down trick both Shadow and I have deployed before. The rest of our team were fascinated by the idea, and I think Hammer is impressed by my wicked maliciousness with this type of attack. It is loud and bold, even for him.

We work together, taking down the websites one by one using exploits in old versions of WordPress or plugins that had been installed on the sites. It was almost child's play, if I am honest. Hammer gets to work on the last of their sites and I turn my attention to the main hosting.

'Glimmer, you and Sarina start to do your thing. Clean our tracks, make us ghosts.'

She nods and they both get to work.

I start to look over the physical hosting. They run a hybrid Windows and Linux system by the looks of it, I assume, to cater for client needs. You have to keep those criminals happy. Seriously, dealing with irate customers when their hosting went down would be bad enough but throw in the fact that they are all of the worlds most wanted criminals you are supporting, downtime for their platforms would not be something you would want to be responsible for or even look like you are responsible for, unless you are Vulcan, of course. They would literally go kill your family if you cost them money. That's just what they do.

For their sake, I would think they would have a pretty solid platform with world-class security, the best you can pay for. Yes, you can't do much about the client's weak update regime, except maybe cover them all with a web access firewall service, stand between them and the world. We already know that isn't the case though. We already wiped out Tareshi's complete web presence.

I don't see any obvious vulnerabilities, but I will just do what I do best and make my way through. Hammer is finished the last site. 'Hammer, why don't you make some noise? Distract them for me for a few minutes while I worm my way in and drop my surprise.'

He smiles. He loves to make noise; he doesn't enjoy sneaking around, doing things quietly like the rest of us do. He likes to be bold. It doesn't take long for him to make an impact; he throws a cyber nuclear attack at the network perimeter protections, a DDOS attack of massive proportions. I can feel their network start to buckle a little before their DDOS protections kick in, reducing the effects.

Hammer turns to look at Sarina's avatar on the main screen. 'Can I get some help?'

She smiles. 'I thought you would never ask.'

Suddenly, the attack is amplified to almost fifty times the initial level. No protection service is going to be able to cope with that very well.

I sneak around, looking for my way in. I can see an exploitable vulnerability on one of the servers, an active directory vulnerability that will allow me to elevate any account to admin privileges. I just need to find myself an active account. I do a quick search for any employees in any of the data breach collections. I grab a couple of them and pipe the credentials into my attack sequence script. I only need one of them to work and then I am in.

I hit execute on the python script, waiting to see if I had any luck. Bingo. I have one. I log in and pivot my access, using the exploit I gain an admin account. I scan the network, looking to see if they have any network segmentation. Nothing – I can see the entire network. They literally have no separation at all. The Windows and Linux platforms are all sitting side by side, just sitting behind the very out of date firewall with operating systems that have barely received any attention in years. It's actually a wonder someone else hasn't popped them yet. I guess it's probably who they host.

The ones who could or would want to hack their systems, all the usual malicious actors, are likely hosted on the same platforms. I guess they are all going to learn in a few more minutes that no one is safe from being hacked, not even the bad guys and girls. The thugs of the digital world. Now they have Vulcan to be scared of. We are on the hunt for them and we will bring as many of them down as we can.

Today is our introduction to the world. Most still won't know we even exist, the bad guys still won't know we exist, just that someone walked through their front door, set the house on fire and then just walked on out without them even knowing what was happening.

Complete destruction – a huge nightmare for both the terrorists and soon their hosts.

I load up my tool. I look around at the team. I can see Hammer just watching me with that look a kid gets when they are standing just outside a lolly shop, the anticipation for something truly amazing. Something wonderous that they know is about to occur. He is waiting for me to burn down the bad guy's house. No, correction: burn down their entire neighbourhood.

I hit execute. The sequence is initiated. Now we watch and wait. Systems start to go offline. My virus is spreading through the network, bringing what remains to its knees. The first part of the mission is complete, time to dig deeper, find anything that is left and erase Tareshi from existence.

'Foresight, I have something you might want to see. Something I captured when cleaning our tracks. I think they might be planning an attack,' Glimmer says.

I get up and go over to her station. I look over the information she is showing me.

'Put it up on the main screens so everyone can see. What does everyone think? Is this credible?'

The team starts to look over the information, analysing what we have.

Shadow is the first to answer. 'It looks credible enough for us to look into it. If it's nothing, all we've lost is time. If it's real, we could have pending attacks imminent. Especially now, after we have just boldly introduced ourselves. If they are planning an attack, they will push forward with more determination than before.'

I nod. I agree with what he is saying and by the looks of the faces of the rest of our team, they agree too. 'Okay, everyone, get to work. Pull every string, find every member. I don't care where they are hiding, we need to know where they are. If this is real, we need to gather this fast. When we know for sure, I will run it up the flagpole.'

They all just get to work. There is no need to talk; we all know what we have to do.

We need to hunt.

CHAPTER 20

CREDIBILITY

The team all look tired. We have been at this for days now. Since we found the whispers of a potential physical attack, the team have been working in shifts, hunting, gathering everything they can. I can tell that we all bear the same level of concern around the situation. The more we dig the more breadcrumbs we find that could point towards a potential terrorist attack, a physical explosion of some kind in both the United States and Australia.

If we go ahead, we will need ASD to handle the allies' communications, have them handle all the US discussions around the potential threat. We will just provide intel. Enough information to allow their teams to find and stop the threats on their soil while we do the same in Australia. We have been able to track most members with around twenty of them still unaccounted for. We need to pin those people down, understand their level of threat.

'Foresight, I've found something. I have some newly issued passports, ones issued within days, all of them have been used to travel overseas. Twelve of them have been scanned on entry to the United States and eight of them have entered Australia via Perth. I am collecting all of the information we have on these and will display them on the main screen,' says DeadlyRose, a hint of concern in her voice.

I turn and look over to the main screen. After a few moments, all twenty identities are up on the screen. We all just look at them for a moment. 'Team, we have our targets. Find them, where they are, where they have been. Everything.

'Sarina, can you monitor all surveillance you can access in Perth? If they pop up anywhere, we need to know about it. I'm going to go talk to the General. It's time he was made aware of the situation.'

Everyone gets to work and I reach down, pulling out my phone from my pocket. I keep forgetting there is no signal down here. I put it back in my pocket and head up to my apartment. When I get there, I take out the phone and find the General's number and hit call. I take a deep breath and just calm myself for the call ahead.

'General, I have a situation you need to be brought up to speed on. We are tracking a potential group of terrorists for the Terishe group. Eight members have entered Australia via Perth and another twelve the United States via New York. From the intel we have gathered, it would appear they may be planning to detonate two explosive devices, one in the US and one in Australia. We are currently searching for them and feel you should reach out to your US counterparts with the twelve identities.'

The phone is silent, with no immediate response. So I continue. 'I will continue to search and then track down both groups while you make contact with the US. If they chose to take over the US side of things, I will shift our focus to our backyard only. We can handle both groups if our assistance is desired though.'

I wait for a few seconds before the General responds. 'You certainly know how to jump into the deep end, don't you? No baby steps in sight for Foresight and her team. Okay, I will reach out to my counterparts and inform them of the details. Send me everything you have on the twelve members who entered the US. Activate secure coms between your team and me so we can communicate as needed.'

'Consider it already done. I will update you as soon as we have located them. It should only be a matter of hours before my team has them in our sights.' The line goes dead and I turn to head back to the lair. 'Sarina, set up secure coms between the General and our team, we will need to keep communication channels open. Send him everything we have on the twenty individuals. Group them in the US and Aus groups so he can easily see which members are in which locations when he passes details over.'

Let's hope that the new core can provide Sarina with the power she needs. We need to be on the ball with this; we need to work fast. Minutes could mean the difference between a major terrorist attack or stopping them before it gets that far. Lives are on the line here, literally.

I walk back into the lair. 'Team, we have opened up communications with ASD. We will be informing them of everything we find. They are reaching out to the US about what we have found. So I know we are all tired but I need our best work on this. Let's get hunting.'

They just nod and get to work. We all know what is needed, no need for pleasantries. It's great to see the team start to come together. They are playing into each other's hands, learning how each works, their styles in the digital world. Every day they are getting better as a team. Right now we need that team, we need a fully operational Vulcan.

Time to find our target and stop them before the worst happens.

CHAPTER 21

THE HUNT

I wonder how long they prepared for this attack or are they just that good at avoiding detection? Since the group left the airport after arriving in Perth, they have barely made an appearance anywhere. Sarina got them a couple of times on a few traffic cameras but then they disappeared, most likely changed cars. We have not been able to tag them anywhere. They are literally like ghosts.

We need to find them somehow. Sarina informed me she has gained access to every camera in the greater Perth area; if they pop up anywhere, she'll find them. She quite literally means everywhere. I see glimpses of bottle shops, ATMs, and traffic cameras. She is watching everything. I am very happy she is on our side; she would be a deadly opponent to try to elude. I honestly don't know if even Shadow and I together could best her, especially with her power upgrades.

'Sarina, keep searching, find them. Everyone else, go get some rest. Once we find them, it'll be all hands on deck again. Take the opportunity while you have it to get some sleep. It may be a while before we get another chance.' None of them argue, leaving the lair as they attempt to hide their yawns behind their hands and stretch their necks, stiff from hours at the keyboards.

Only Shadow remains behind leaning against his desk, waiting for me. 'You need to get some rest too, I haven't seen you take a single break,' he says. 'Sarina can handle the search and let us know when she has anything. Isn't that right, Sarina?' He steps closer to me, sliding his hands over my hips. I get a tingling sensation; it's like his touch electrifies my every nerve.

'Of course I can handle that. Both of you need to go do your human stuff. I will inform you as soon as I have anything to report.'

I guess he is right, we should both get some rest. Get ready for what is to come next.

'I will take this chance to take a shower and get some sleep since everything is under control.' I think all Shadow heard in that statement was me going to take a shower. Is he picturing me taking the shower? He's completely zoned out. I jab him in the ribs. 'Mind out of the gutter, Shadow.'

He smiles a little sheepishly. Yep, he was definitely picturing me naked.

I turn and head to the elevator and he follows my lead. When we get into the elevator, he turns to look at me with a cheeky smile. 'Would you like some company in the shower?'

The elevator door opens – it's Shadow's floor. He's facing me with his back to the doors, so I walk forward, gently pushing him back out of the elevator.

'I think you need a nice cold shower. On your own.' I step back, allowing the elevator doors to close between us. But my mind starts to imagine if I had taken him up on his offer. What would it be like with Shadow and I in the shower? My mind wanders, thinking of his touch, the electricity between us. I need to stop these thoughts or I am never going to get any sleep tonight. Maybe I should have a cold shower myself.

I head straight for a shower. It makes me feel all refreshed and relaxed. I lay down on the bed and drift off to sleep.

'Foresight, I have something,' Sarina says.

I snap awake, it's been five hours. Wow, that went fast.

'I will be right down.'

Mmmm, maybe after I get dressed. I didn't even put any clothes on after the shower. I had just laid back, thinking I would just rest for a few minutes and was out to it in seconds. I grab some clothes, getting dressed quickly, fixing my hair in the reflective surface in the lift.

I walk through to see a video on screen with one of our suspects. Sarina is tracking him through multiple video feeds, satellite and is pinging phones from all the nearby phone towers. By the looks of things, she is trying to narrow down the number that is his, one that is following his path. She is getting close.

'I have been tracking him for around thirty minutes now. I haven't pinpointed any of the others yet but I will. Do you want me to wake the others?'

I think about it for a few moments. 'No, let them sleep, we can handle this until we get something more to work on.'

On the screen, she has fixated on one number, our suspect's number.

'Sarina, can you see where that phone was purchased and if any others were purchased at the same time?'

Another window jumps up with the purchase location: a Telstra shop in one of the suburbs. Seven other phones were also bought in that same transaction.

'Sarina, track the locations of all eight numbers on that purchase. We need to know where they all are, at all times.'

Sarina loads a map and starts to pinpoint the phones. Some of them grouped, but others are spread around the country.

'We need to figure out what they have planned, we need to watch everything they do.'

What could they be after? They've spread out. Some of them are on the Sunshine Coast in Queensland, Sydney in New South Wales and some remain in Perth. What is in these locations that would be of high enough value for them to strike? What is the end game here? I don't understand what the angle is here.

We watch them for a few more hours. They seem to be collecting equipment. Getting ready for whatever it is they are going to do. All we can do is watch and be ready for whatever it is. Once we have the target we can move in and stop it. Hopefully shut them down before it gets too far, once we have some proof of what they intend to do.

'Sarina, share the updated information with the General. It's time they got some boots on the ground and prepared for a response when it is needed.'

I see them collecting diving equipment. What could they want with diving equipment? None of this situation makes any sense to me. These three locations having nothing critical, there are no upcoming major events in the coming days in all locations. What are they doing? There has to be a simple explanation, something that we don't understand, a missing piece to this puzzle.

CHAPTER 22
TARGETS

The whole team is back in the lair. We have been watching the suspects go about their business. Sarina has video and satellite surveillance on all of them. She is tracking their phones. We are monitoring all communications. Well, actually we are monitoring no communications because they aren't communicating with each other at all, not even data traffic from the phones. Not a single thing. They are all doing their parts, of what exactly though, that is the big question. What are they planning for?

'We need to figure out what they are doing, what is important about these three places, what connects them all together, if anything at all? What are we are missing?'

The team looks over what we know, what Sarina and the team now understand. They are all collecting diving gear, they have rented boats, decent size boats. Why? What are they all going to do in the water?

'Foresight,' Hammer says, his brow furrowed as if he has a theory. 'All of these locations have one thing in common and the diving gear would make sense if my theory is right.' He pauses, he looks as though he is not sure if he should say it, like he is second-guessing himself.

'Well, let us have the theory,' I say.

He looks up at me for a moment. 'Have we considered the

submarine lines that connect us to the rest of the world? All three locations are landing points for these submarine fibre links. The newest is at the Sunshine Coast.'

'Hammer, I think you could be on to something. Your theory would explain the diving equipment. What are they intending to do though?'

He gets a huge grin like he is a child answering a tough question thrown out to the class by a teacher.

Glimmer looks puzzled. 'How would they benefit from accessing the cables? Is it data they want, do they want to spy on us? It doesn't make sense. There has to be something else, something bigger that we are not seeing.'

Shadow taps his pen on his desk, a look of concentration pinching his brows. 'This type of disruption could just be a distraction, allowing them to enact a bigger attack, cut us off from the world, destroy the fibre links and then hit us hard somehow.'

Shadow is probably right, there is more to this, but we can't allow them to take out these cables. We need to ensure we are ready to stop them before that happens.

'I need you to get me something more concrete than a theory. We need to start preparing the teams for a strike, to take them out before they can cause any disruption.'

The team gets to work, all searching for breadcrumbs in each other's artifacts, anything anyone has missed. It's interesting to watch code moving around the screens with images and documents. To an outsider it may look chaotic but it has a rhythm, a style, each of us have our own footprint, you could call it. A sort of hacker fingerprint.

We are looking for anything that can prove our theory or even disprove it so we can move on. We need to follow the true path the data takes us, no matter that trajectory.

I get to work myself, looking for breadcrumbs, clues that could validate everything.

I hear someone walk up behind me; it is DeadlyRose. 'I have what we need. A communication we captured in the first mission with the group is design documents for what looks to be a ring explosive device. It would appear they are going to place them around the cables and destroy them.' She shares the documentation on the big screen. She is right: this is the final piece of evidence we need, the one that strings it all together.

'We need to find out how they are going to get those explosive devices. Do they have them already? It would make more sense if they already had them before they went their separate ways. We need to find them and strike the targets before they can get into position.'

I still feel that niggling feeling, like we are missing something… So they are going to cut off Australia's connection to the outer world or at least slow it down. We still have satellite communications, albeit very slow compared to the fibre submarine links, but still, they can be used to maintain primary communications.

Is this just a distraction? What else do they have planned? Something we need to figure out before it literally blows up in our faces.

We keep digging for what seems like hours. We have a few interactions and some minor discussions about things that someone has found but nothing of real consequence. We need to solve this and shut it down.

Sarina interrupts my thoughts. 'Foresight, two of the members have gone dark. I can not find where they have gone. It is like they just vanished.'

I look at the map Sarina has put on the screen. Our missing terrorists are both from the Sydney cluster, leaving just one left. Is this the warning they are getting ready to strike or have they caught on we are watching them?

'The remaining teams are getting into position. They are all boarding their boats. What do you want to do?'

Do we wait and see where the two remaining members are, get the whole team, or do we take them down now? I don't think we have much choice.

'Sarina, inform the General it's time to strike. It's time to take them out before they have a chance to do any damage. We will need to find the last two members though. We can't have any loose ends once we strike. Keep an eye on the active members, Sarina. The rest of you, find the others.'

CHAPTER 23

PREPARE TO STRIKE

It's 4 a.m. and we have been watching the terrorists start to make their move. They have loaded their boats and have headed out onto the coastline, just out from where the cables land in their respective locations. We have acquired several satellites and are watching each of the groups. We still haven't located the missing two members, but we have the six locked in our sights. They have all dropped anchor and are readying themselves to drop into the water.

We have Australian naval ships and water police standing by just out of sight in all three locations. Specialised SEAL teams are on board and ready to breach the target vessels as soon as we give the all-clear. I would prefer to know what the other two players on the table are doing, our missing pieces, before we take them out, but I am running out of time.

'Sarina, any progress on our search? Have they popped up anywhere?' I look at the info on our screens and nothing has changed. I can see the satellite imagery of our targets; the team is tracing back through the information we have, building the evidence we need.

'No change, Foresight. They are still dark.'

'Team, do you have anything new? Do we have a reason not to strike? Or is it a go?'

They all look at each other and Shadow answers. 'We have nothing of value, more evidence to confirm what they intend to do with our submarine lines, nothing on what the plan is with our remaining two members here in Australia. Should we share intel with the US counterparts on what they are doing even though they have not asked for assistance? It could be of value to them.'

I guess the decision is on my shoulders. With nothing further to go on, I need to make a judgement call. The logical choice would be to take out the current threat, deal with the other two once that is done. 'Sarina, inform the teams to move in, take out the targets. Also share the terrorist targets with our counterparts, tell them what we have found out. It may help them on their end.'

The teams at each location get into position as we watch on the surveillance cameras, readying themselves for the pending mission. I am intrigued to see how the teams do. They are using a combination of attack boats and jet packs. It's crazy to think jet packs are a thing. They are a thing of sci-fi movies, not reality, but here they are. I've seen them in YouTube videos for a few years, people testing them out, but the fact that the military has workable assault options with these is just crazy.

Each unit has two armed soldiers with jet packs and another eight members on the two boarding boats – well, if that's what you would call them. They are completely enclosed vessels that when in operation glide along just below the surface, like mini jet boats or submarines. I have never seen anything like these before. It's like something you would seriously see in a Batman or James Bond movie. I am going to enjoy watching them work.

I was told during mission prep they use the vessels in missions where stealth is of utmost importance, allowing them to essentially pounce on their targets without warning. It is amazing how quickly what once was only sci-fi can become reality.

The jet pack members get into position on the respecting decks of each of the ships and the soldiers boarding the jet boats, securing the hulls.

'Vulcan, do we still have a go? We are in position and ready to move on the targets,' the team leader asks.

I clear my thoughts. 'You have a go.'

The boats take off, disappearing into the water, almost invisible to the eye, although I know where they are. Moments later, the jet packs take off, hurling like a freight train towards our targets. The room is quiet, everyone is watching, almost holding their breath. If you studied the screens close enough, you could see the boats breach the surface slightly when cutting through waves. They are very fast, closing the gap on their targets quickly. It will be only a few moments before they're in a position to board the target's boats.

They approach from different sides, slowing as they near their target, allowing the doors on the top of the boats to open as they get within a few metres. The jet packs come in from the top, and within a few seconds, it's all over. The jet pack riders land, clearing the way for the soldier's entry, washing over each side like a wave. The terrorists never know it's coming until it is too late and they are overwhelmed before they get a chance to consider a reaction.

Just like that, it is over.

'Vulcan, all targets are secure. Explosive devices deactivated. The main vessels are en route and evidence will be collected as required. If we find anything, we will inform you immediately.'

I look around at the team. 'Good work, team. We have done a great service today for our country, but this isn't over. We need to find the two missing members, find out what they have planned. I have a bad feeling about them. They have something big planned and we need to find out what that it is.'

CHAPTER 24

MISDIRECTION

The rest of the day went smoothly. All the evidence had been collected. Terrorists were sent off for interrogation at one of ASD's black holes. I'm not sure if we will ever see them again, but I hope the interrogators can get something of value from them, some piece of information that could help us find their friends. I fear that it will be too late by the time we get anything of value though. Something bad is coming, but what?

I sent the team to get some rest. They did a great job and deserve a couple of hours of sleep. Shadow stayed with me. We've been looking over the evidence trying to find our needle in a haystack, as they say. Anything that will lead us to the missing terrorists.

'Foresight, I have found something, something you need to see. I think I may have just found out what their plan is.'

Shadow is watching something unfold on one of the news channels. It looks like we are too late.

The scene is a mess of fire and metal. It looks like cars that have been blown up, bullet holes in them and the surroundings. What the hell is this? Who is the target? The attack was in Canberra, a government motorcade by the looks. Who was inside though? It looks like a battle zone, one you would see in Iran or Iraq, or somewhere like that, not on Australian streets.

'Sarina, get us everything on what just happened. Is this our people? Who was the target?' It looks like the police are mobilising at the scene, cordoning the area off. Bodies are everywhere, it's a sickening sight.

'Foresight, this is bad. The target was the Prime Minister. He has been taken and they don't know if he is alive or not at this stage. The targets have fled the scene and are currently off-grid. They are nowhere to be found.'

Oh crap. Our team allowed the Prime Minister to be taken on our own soil. Wow, this might be a very short stint for Vulcan. We need to get him back in one piece and shut these terrorists down.

'Sarina, get the team back down to the lair, all hands on deck. Shadow, I think you need to give Deano a call. If we find the Prime Minister, we want the best to get him out safely. We can't have any mistakes.'

The whole fibre lines were just a misdirection, they were never the primary targets. Yes, they would have made some noise and certainly distracted us. They had a bigger fish in mind. How could they even get that close to him? How could they know where he was going to be? This shouldn't happen.

'Foresight, I have the General on the line for you. He doesn't sound happy.'

This is going to suck. 'Sarina, put him through.' I get up, walking away from my team so I am out of earshot and tap my earpiece. 'Sir.'

The line is silent for a few moments. 'We are in a bit of a situation, Sam. I need you to resolve this immediately. You are the best team we have. Find the Prime Minister and get him back. I don't care how or what you need to do to get him back, just do it. Whatever you need, it is yours.'

'We will do our best, sir. You have my word.'

The General's response is almost instant. 'Make some noise,

Foresight. Show these sons of bitches that this is not something that happens in Australia.'

Then he is gone. I hear the lair door opening and the rest of the team is back. They look a little ruffled; they don't know what has happened. 'The Prime Minister has been taken by the two remaining terrorists. The fibre links weren't the primary target – he was. We've been given the authorisation to make some noise, do whatever is necessary to secure his safe return. So, let's do what we do best.'

I can see by the looks on the team's faces they were not expecting that. I don't blame them. I'm still not sure it has sunk in for me yet either. Things like this just don't happen in Australia. I see Shadow return from having a phone conversation at the back of the lair, I assume to Deano.

He walks straight to my side. 'Deano says he is ready when we need him. We just need to get his team into place, and they'll get him out.'

That's good to hear. They are the best there is and we need the best right now.

The team gets to work piecing the event back together, figuring out how the kidnapping was able to occur. It was very well planned, I will give the terrorists that. They took their captive two streets down and swapped vehicles. A blue SUV.

'Sarina, track that SUV. We need to know every move it makes. Shadow, I need you to commandeer all available Loyal Wingman prototype drones. They have been building a fleet of these for defence in Queensland and they have some pretty advanced tech that will come in handy with tracking the Prime Minister's location. They will also have quite a bit of firepower to help get him out safely if Deano's team needs a bit of support. Sarina, we might need your help to control all of the drones once we have control of them.'

Shadow nods. 'I know them, that's a good idea. I'll get onto it now.

Clarification, is this a friendly takeover? Or do you want me to do it the hard way?'

I smile. I think he would enjoy the challenge of hacking them, breaking the war machines of the sky. If I am honest, I think I would probably enjoy the challenge myself but we don't have time for that.

'I'll call the General. Expect a call in a few minutes with everything you need.'

He nods again. 'Roger that.'

I walk away from my desk. 'Sarina, connect me to the General.' It only takes a few moments.

'What do you need, Sam?' He's straight to the point, as always.

'I need the Loyal Wingman. All of them that are available, fully loaded and in the air, under our control.'

The line is quiet for a moment. 'You want to put the most advanced and lethal planes we have available fully loaded into Australian airspace with no oversight?'

I guess it is a big ask. 'You did say whatever I needed, sir.'

He laughs. 'Yes, I guess I did. Expect a call in a few minutes. You'll have what you need.'

I can only imagine what people are going to think with stealth drones flying around above the city. We don't have time to do this quietly though. We need to find the PM and get him out.

The General is right. It only takes a few minutes before he transfers through a call to me from Boeing Defence with authorisation to take over all units for a live-fire assault. We have access to six Loyal Wingmen immediately with the team prepping two more for reserve if needed.

I transfer them over to Shadow, who is getting us all set up with the encryption channels and secure command portals. Once they are in our control, we will hand them over to Sarina to manage them, with Shadow giving primary direction as he always is. I can see Sarina has tracked the targets through two more vehicles swaps. We are starting to narrow down the location.

It is almost time to hunt.

CHAPTER 25

LOYAL WINGMEN AND THE GROUND CRAWLERS

The six Loyal Wingmen have come online, and they are en route to Canberra's air space. Shadow has informed me that Deano and his team are now en route to Canberra, with help from our new Boeing friends. They have with them some top-secret armoured vehicles that Boeing Defence have been working on as ground support units for the Loyal Wingmen. They are fully loaded and will also be controlled by Sarina to get Deano and his team in and out of the assault. It helps when you have a direct order coming from the top of the food chain telling them to give you everything you need and now.

Sarina is still tracking the group. The vehicle they are travelling with is heading out into the country. We will track them until we get a final resting place.

'Sarina, when the drones get into position keep them at a height that will not allow them to be detected. Just use them to do reconnaissance and to make sure we don't have any surprises.'

We continue to watch them for another hour, just keeping in a holding pattern, preparing for what is going to come next. It's midafternoon now and it will probably be nighttime before we are ready to strike and confirm the final target.

'Team, we need to be ready. Whatever comes next, we need to

bring our A-game, this is our prime minister they have. We need to have a swift rescue then we need to finish off this group; no matter what they have left, it needs to be obliterated. This needs to be a loud message, one that can be heard around the world, one that tells everyone Australia is off-limits. You hit us, we'll hit back with ten times the force. The General wants it to be loud, so let's be loud.'

'Foresight, the targets are coming to a stop. It looks likes some sort of old warehouse. They are not alone though – there looks to be a small army. I will get the wingmen in position and use the infrared capability to detect all targets,' says Sarina.

I see the drones form a holding pattern, allowing Sarina to get every angle of the facility and she starts to form a cohesive map of the site. We have what looks to be twenty to twenty-five people. One of which would be the prime minister.

This is going to get very loud.

That's a big task for Deano and his team, but they do have a lot of support from the Wingmen and ground crawlers. Well, that's the name I'm giving them. With the eight vehicles and the six planes, it is going to look like a massive force is heading their way.

'How far away is Deano's team?'

A few moments go by before Sarina gives a response. 'I am tracking their heavy transport, it is only minutes away. They will land the Chinooks a few kilometres away to ensure they don't draw any attention.' Chinook helicopters. Wow, they have brought out all the stops to get our team what they need.

It's almost dark and the vehicles are all black so they will be hard to see in the low light. They don't need to use lights; they are all autonomous vehicles controlled by sensors and radar. The occupants and my team can see night vision footage direct from the units, but the vehicles themselves don't need it.

As soon as they are on the ground, we need to get them ready to make a breach. It will need to be swift and stealthy initially. We don't want them to know what is coming until we are upon them. They could panic and kill the prime minister before we can get to him. None of us wants that to happen. That would be what you would call the worst possible result and the end of my team, that is for sure.

I can see the chinooks landing on the satellite coverage. Eight vehicles drive out and immediately start to head towards their targets. One of them is carrying our team; they will stay in the middle of the pack until they are ready to strike. Two will accompany the team to their breach location, with the other five taking up strategic attack positions. The Chinooks wind down. They don't take off again – they will stay ready for a quick exit if needed.

'Sarina, we need to determine the likely location of the prime minister so the team can hit the facility and get him out as quickly as possible. Once they have him, we will open the building up with the ground crawlers and get him out. They can smash their way through the warehouse doors, windows, from all directions. Once they are outside, the Loyal Wingmen can clear the path to safety.'

Details of the site have been sent to the ground team and they are coming over the hill towards the facility now. 'Vulcan lair, we are in position, awaiting your command.' Deano's voice always fills me with confidence.

I look at the information on the screens and scan the faces of our team; they all look ready. A serious, determined look on each of their faces. 'Sarina, do we have a location?'

Silence fills the air for what feels like minutes but in reality was more likely just seconds before Sarina responds. 'Location determined. We are ready to go'.

'Ground crawlers are a go. Get in and out safe, team.'

There is no response from the team, they just surge into action. Sarina divides the units, sending them in all directions. The three strike vehicles head directly to a side entrance, driving straight over a security fence like it wasn't even there.

They are running quiet, barely a sound, as all units take their positions. I can see on the screen the targeting systems are collecting targeting information, ready to take out the targets when the breach occurs. The two escort vehicles split off to the sides as they near the building, allowing for the primary vehicle to edge closer to the target. The crawler comes to a stop and the back ramp opens up allowing for Deano and his crew to exit before closing up again. It retreats slightly taking up a defensive position.

They breach the building quietly, making their way in towards where the prime minister should be. Everything is quiet, barely a guard patrol. Something doesn't feel right. Are we sending our team into a trap? Or do the terrorists think they have gotten away with this? No one knows where they are. We watch the feeds from the body cameras. It's pretty dark, and they are sticking to the shadows.

Then I see him. The prime minister is in some sort of makeshift cell on one side of the building. He looks a little worse for wear. I don't think he was completely unscathed in the assault that took him.

I glance up at the Loyal Wingmen feeds. Wait. What? There are a large number of men moving in around the team. They are setting up a trap.

'It's a trap! They are surrounding the team as we speak. Sarina, bring in the ground crawlers, breach the facility and protect the team. Time to use the Loyal Wingmen to clear their exit. Time to go loud.'

The crawlers all move into position and prepare to breach every side. They are going to come at the enemy from all sides. 'Ground crawlers, you are about to have a lot of company. We are sending in reinforcements. Secure the package and get the hell out of there.'

'Copy that, Vulcan lair. Time to go loud.'

At that, I see the ground crawlers firing missiles and driving straight through the damaged walls, bullets flying everywhere as they move into position surrounding our team, creating a shield wall around them and the prime minister. Deano makes a move and gets the prime minister out of the cell. He looks in bad shape, but in good spirits. I assume that has something to do with his pretty dramatic rescue team. The back opens on one of the ground crawlers, allowing for the team to carry him into safety. 'The package is secure. Time to get the hell out of here.'

'Sarina, you heard the man, clear the road!'

Instantly, explosions go off everywhere, the drones taking out all the target's assets. The attack ensures there is no resistance for our exit once we reach the open air. Bullets are flying, grenades are going off – they are trying everything to stop the crawlers from getting out of the building. But they have been made for just this scenario. They are going to need to do a lot better than that.

I hear Shadow giving Sarina instructions. Suddenly the weapons on all the crawlers start to target the terrorists. They quickly take down almost fifteen men and push forward. As they do, they flank the crawler with the team on board.

It only takes a few seconds and they break out through one side of the building. It looks like a warzone – explosions, gunfire, it's chaos.

'Sarina, once the team is clear, surround the facility and ensure no one leaves. Call in a clean-up team and secure anyone who is still alive,' I say. One of the Loyal Wingmen and the two escort crawlers stay with the team as they dash back to the Chinooks. The remaining units fall into watch positions, returning fire to any combatants that engage them. I don't think there is going to be much left for the clean-up crew.

'Ground crawlers, what is the status of the package?'

A few moments go by before we get an answer. 'The package is secure and is in good health. He will make a full recovery.'

The smiles on the team's faces are wide. We did it, the prime minister is safe.

'Deano, once the package is safe, make your way to Brisbane. I want to discuss a more permanent arrangement with you and your team.'

'Copy that, Vulcan lair. See you soon.'

I turn to the team. 'Let's finish this.'

CHAPTER 26

MAKING A STATEMENT

The team has been hard at work, hunting down any remaining members of the group. We want to end this for good, with no chance of further incidents. That means we needed to overstep our jurisdiction a little by tracking down the members of the group who entered the US. We already had the groundwork done so it was just a matter of letting DeadlyRose do her thing. We found the breadcrumbs and let her follow them to the targets. Once we had them in our sights, we engaged our US counterparts and watched as they were taken down one by one.

I was surprised by how smoothly and quickly we could make it happen. We were lucky the US terrorist team was still very much in the preparation stages, collecting weapons and vehicles. It would appear they were planning a similar snatch up of a US official, but we are not sure on the exact target, something I am sure the FBI will be looking to glean from the captured terrorists.

Any remaining digital trace of the group has been scrubbed from the internet. I don't want even a whisper of them left. Almost like they had never existed. It is strange that we could do such a thing, erase a group from existence, only to remain in memory for those who witnessed their crimes against humankind.

As I take down their last site, I look around and see the team.

They are all tired but happy. They look like they know they have done a good thing today. As a team, we did well today. We made a difference in a world that can be hard to affect, one that would normally be impossible to change due to red tape and politics. We stood apart from all of that and just got on with the job. We didn't ask permission, just reacted and changed course as needed. Vulcan has truly become the team I knew we could become. We can now stand as one, as Vulcan together.

'Why don't you all go get some rest? I'll finish up here.'

They nod and finish what they are doing then slowly, one by one, make their way out of the lair, leaving just Shadow and I, as is becoming normal. 'You too, Shadow.'

He looks at me. 'I can't very well leave before the boss does. How is that going to look? I need to stay in the good books, remember.'

He really is a great guy. A lot of men would have an issue with having a female boss, especially one as young as I am; he doesn't seem to mind it at all. Maybe its partly to do with his feelings for me. I love having him as a part of my team. To think a few months ago we were enemies; I was hunting him. I don't think any of us could have predicted this would be how things would have turned out, us working together, doing what we do best.

'Very well. You can finish the mop-up then while I go check in with the General.'

He nods and gets to work. I love how he never questions my direction, never seems to make any judgement about my decisions, just gets on with his job, whatever I have asked of him.

'Sarina, please connect me to the General.'

A few seconds later, the call comes through my earpiece. 'Foresight, I was just wondering when you were going to check in. You have done a great service today. Ensure you thank that team of yours for all the hard work. The prime minister is doing well and will be released tonight thanks to your team. He wanted me to personally thank you all for your assistance and indicated that if you or anyone in the Vulcan team needs help, a favour from him, consider it done.'

That's a good favour to have in your arsenal: the prime minister's ear or no questions asked approval. People would kill for a favour of that kind. All we had to do was take on a terrorist group, wage war on hostile hostage-takers, and control the most advanced military force in Australia fully loaded onto and over federal land. I think that would have to be an Australian first. Well, the first I've ever heard of.

'He'll be doing a statement tonight as he leaves the hospital, one that may entice some backlash, so make sure your team gets some rest. You might be very busy again tomorrow. He's going to publicly call out the group and state that Australia took them down. He is going to tell the world that Australia is off-limits; if you come at us, we will retaliate. We will stand tall and defend our way of life.' He pauses for a moment before continuing. 'As you would expect, I have advised him against this path but he has agreed to keep your team out of it to protect your cover.'

Well, that's going to be a big statement. The equivalent of standing up and saying, 'Try harder, you stupid terrorist. I am not down, I am not finished, I am just getting started.' I like his style. Risky and not something you would normally see from an Australian prime minister, but good on him. After what he just went through, you have to be impressed, having the guts to still stand up, straight and proud. Like a true Australian.

'Thank you, General. I will pass that onto my team. I've sent them all to get some rest, ready for our next mission.'

I can hear him laugh slightly. 'You just saved the leader of our country from imminent death and you are already thinking of your next move. Make sure you take a bit of downtime for yourself, you've earned it. Maybe return those borrowed toys before too many questions get asked though.'

Now I laugh. 'Consider it done. Goodnight, General.'

The line goes quiet; he has gone.

He is right, I should take this opportunity to take some downtime, enjoy myself a little. I look over at Shadow. I think it's time for me to find out what this thing between us is going to be. I feel the butterflies start to stir, the familiar rush of adrenaline pushing through my body. I walk over to him and sit on the desk beside him. I wait for him to look up at me. As he does, I smile. 'Well, the bosses are happy.'

He smiles. 'That's good to hear. I have just finished the last of the clean-up. We are done.'

The mission is done. No more to do except wait and see what the reaction is from the press conference. Will it entice a newfound threat, a new enemy? I think I will leave that as tomorrow's problem.

'Tomorrow night, a date, you and I. We will go out to dinner, the whole thing. You in?' I ask him.

A smile lights up his face. 'Am I in? I wouldn't miss it for the world. I'll meet you in the foyer downstairs at 7 p.m?'

I smile now and start to get up off the desk.

'Tomorrow, 7 p.m. in the foyer. Done.'

CHAPTER 27

RETURNING THE TOYS

After the mop-up was done and all the remaining terrorist members had been captured, the ground crawlers had all been loaded back into the Chinooks and headed back to Brisbane. Sarina had kept the Loyal Wingmen monitoring the area for a few more hours, just in case anyone had slipped through. None had so the planes were redirected back to their home base with all units back in Boeing's hands before sunup. Only minor damage to any of the ground units and no damage at all for the air team. A great result, considering what we have just accomplished with them in the last twenty-four hours.

The prime minister's press conference went smoothly; the media ate it up. The whole being taken hostage and defiantly telling the world Australia is off-limits will definitely help him at the polls. He is now a hero of the people, our way of life. It's all you can see anyone talking about across the media. There hasn't been any backlash as yet. I have a bad feeling about it though. Something is coming, I can feel it.

I have some loose ends to tie up before my date. I am getting ready to take a trip out to Boeing's base of operations, to take stock of any damage and to provide a personal thank you to the team for lending us their toys to play with. I am told they have some questions about the units, how they reacted during use, any issues. It was their first real-life assault test, so they'll want to learn as much as they can about how it all went to iron out any issues.

I have told Sarina to prepare a full report on how they functioned, any bugs or issues she found during her operation of them in the mission, as well as any suggestions on the platform that may improve either their operating software or their physical functionality. She has already provided me with an eighty-page report with detailed feedback and suggestions including some code fixes to improve bugs. These guys are going to wonder who the hell we are and how the hell have we been able to do so much in a short period. I will need to be careful not to reveal Sarina. It might not be safe for her if I do.

'Sarina, can you prepare some transport to take me to the Boeing facility? It's time to go shake some hands.'

I make my way downstairs and out through the front foyer area. I suddenly feel like I am being watched; the hairs on my arms are standing up on end. 'Sarina, is there anyone else in my vicinity?' I ask softly.

Her response is instant. 'Affirmative. A heat signature is approaching your left-hand side, in three, two, one. They are right beside you now.'

I glide my hand down to clasp my pistol, unclipping it as I do.

I turn, ready to respond to the threat and I see Shadow just standing there less than a metre away looking at me. I relax, taking my hand from my gun, resecuring it as I do.

'Sorry if I spooked you. Are you going somewhere, boss? Do you need some company?'

'Yes, I have a thank you to deliver to Boeing for letting us borrow their expensive toys. I figured it was the least I could do. No escort needed, I got this.'

He looks me in the eyes for a few moments before taking a step closer. I can see the car pull up just in front of us. 'Are we still on for tonight?'

I smile a little. So that's what he is concerned about, our date tonight.

'Yes, we are still on tonight.' I step forward and open the driver's door of the vehicle, but before I get in, I turn back to Shadow. 'Don't get into any trouble while I'm gone. I will see you tonight.'

I get in and Sarina starts to drive. The trip doesn't take long. We pull up at the security gate and introduce myself saying that I am expected. The guard steps into his booth to check my authority to enter the facility and after a few seconds apologises to me and immediately opens the gate.

'Please head directly to the main building in front of you, ma'am. The director of defence projects will meet you just inside the foyer area.'

I nod, acknowledging the guard's statement. 'Thank you.'

Sarina starts heading towards the building as directed.

'Sarina, you should keep a low profile while we are here. I am not sure we should reveal you to anyone outside of our team just yet.' The place is crawling with guards. It's a very high-security site; I wonder what else they are working on here, what the rest of the world has no idea about.

Sarina responds through the cars speakers. 'Affirmative, Foresight. Low profile it is. Would you like me to stay in your ear in case I am needed? Or should I stay dark until your return to the vehicle?'

I consider for a moment. I will assume they are monitoring the signals, anything electronic. 'Probably best to stay dark until my return.' The car stops in a park just outside the building and I start to get out of the vehicle. 'I won't be very long.'

I remove the earpiece and put it in the door storage area and close the door behind me. It is going to be weird without Sarina in my ear. She's been there almost the whole time since Vulcan was formed.

I walk up to the two front doors and they open in front of me to reveal a small group of people waiting for me just inside. I step forward, closing the gap between us until I am just a few metres away. One of them steps forward, extending his hand. I shake his hand with a firm grip, like my father always taught me to do. I can hear his words in my head: *A firm handshake. Looking someone in the eyes is how you show respect and that you are someone who should be respected.*

'Foresight, is it? The leader of Vulcan? That's your unit's name, isn't it?'

I let go of his hand. 'Yes, that is correct.'

He smiles. 'I am Jack Buyer, director of defence projects, and this is the lead for the Loyal Wingmen project that includes the ground support. I believe you have dubbed them Ground Crawlers? We like the name and will be adopting it. I hope you don't mind.'

I smile. 'They're your toys, you can call them whatever you like. I hope we have returned them in an adequate state.'

He nods. 'A few minor scratches on the ground fleet but worth it for the data and feedback your team has already given us. The team has been reviewing it this morning and is already taking steps to introduce the adjustments your team has suggested. They will all be better for the adjustments.'

I nod. 'I'm glad you have found it useful.'

He gestures for me to follow him down the corridor so I follow as directed. 'We noticed some external code on the systems, some adjustments that had been made on the fly. It's very creative coding, you have a very impressive team. How many of you are there?' He is a little suspicious. He doesn't understand how we could have done what we have done in such a short amount of time.

'We are a small team, but I can't reveal exact numbers.'

He nods. 'Yes, of course, apologies.' He continues to walk to the back of the building and we approach a set of high-security doors. After scanning his palm print and retina to access the area, we continue through the doors. On either side of the doors as we go through there are armed soldiers. They look like defence guys. As I look around the room there are many more positioned around the area. They really want to protect this stuff.

'We would like to offer your team a deal, of sorts, if you are interested.'

I look around as we walk through into an open area. It looks like a plane hanger big enough to house twenty planes. Some of the wingmen and ground crawlers have been parked here with people with what look like lab coats looking over them, diagnostic equipment plugged into their control systems. Over the back of the facility in the direction we are walking, I can see some sort of helicopter and a fleet of SUVs.

'What sort of deal are we talking about?' I've never seen anything like the helicopter cross drone cross apache helicopter. It looks really wicked. It is matte black and looks as though it can carry up to six passengers in a very luxurious looking cockpit. The SUV's are matte black and look real tough. They are all darkened out and I can't see inside. They look like they could drive through a wall like the ground crawlers though. Just a little less military and more luxury limousine style look.

'We have been working on some executive transport, heavily armoured, semi-autonomous and very capable. They make that Tesla out the front look like a kid's toy in comparison. They have all of the capability of the crawlers but in a nice-to-look-at package for street cruising. What do you think?'

I walk over to the closest vehicle to me and climb into the driver's seat, which on the inside looks more like a cockpit. Monitors and display panels are everywhere around me. It looks like the vehicle can hold six people in comfort. Jack walks up to the passenger side of the vehicle and talks to me through the open door. 'We are looking at a modified version of these being built for the prime minister after the recent attack to ensure it can't occur again. We wanted to see if your team could use an advanced set of vehicles to – how would I put it – road test the abilities, provide us with some real-world feedback. Really put the units through their paces. It seems like that is something Vulcan would be quite capable of doing.'

I run my hands over the steering wheel, just taking it all in. They do look very capable and would be good assets to have available if needed.

'What's the catch? What do you get out of it?' I ask.

He climbs into the passenger seat and looks at me straight in the eyes. 'We get your team. We have some of the best engineers in the world building these systems and if we want to ensure that our systems are the best, we need to ensure they are put through the paces, really tested and bugs ironed out by the best. From what I see and what my engineers are telling me, that is your team.'

'What about maintenance and repairs when they are used on missions. Do you look after that? We just provide feedback and improvement suggestions.'

He nods. 'Yes, we will maintain and provide your team with the latest equipment, the best of everything we have. If things don't work right or aren't up to scratch, tell us what you need and we will make it happen.'

It sounds like a pretty good deal.

'What about that helicopter thing you have there. Do we get one of those as well?'

He smiles at me. 'It is pretty impressive, isn't it?' He looks out the window at one of his team who nods. 'Yes, I think we can make that happen.'

I nod and climb out of the vehicle, walking back around to stand next to the remaining team. 'I will discuss this with my team and if they have no issues with any of this, we have a deal.'

Jack looks very pleased with my response, rubbing his hands together with what appears to be excitement. 'Perfect, I am happy to hear it.' He gestures for me to walk with him back the way we came. We exchange some general chitchat along the way. As we get to the foyer area again, he stops and offers me his hand. 'It was a true pleasure meeting you, Foresight. I hope we have a great partnership moving forward and if you need anything at all, let me know we have authority from the top to help your team in any way we can.'

I shake his hand and make my way back out to the car. It unlocks as I approach and I climb in. I pick up the earpiece and immediately hear Sarina's voice.

'Are we good?' she asks.

I pull my seatbelt on. 'Yes, let's get out of here. Looks like the team is going to be getting some cool new toys to play with. Some more tech for you to iron out all the kinks with.'

We head back towards the guard gate and the barrier is lifted as we get closer.

'Take us home, Sarina. Make sure we aren't followed though, just to be safe.'

CHAPTER 28

DATE NIGHT

I get back to our building around lunchtime. We took the long route back with a few backtracks to ensure we were not followed. It's nothing personal against our new friends – I trust very few people in this world. There is always some sort of protection in place, especially after my snatch and grab. I'm wired to be suspicious about everything and everyone. My choice of career probably doesn't help that either.

Sarina takes the car into the car park downstairs, and I wait until she confirms the area is clear before I exit the vehicle.

'Sarina, inform the General of the offer from our new friends and confirm if he has any concerns or issues with the arrangement.'

I walk up to the elevator and head upstairs. I make myself something for lunch and just chill out on the couch with a good movie. I end up watching two and when I look over at the clock it's almost 5:30 p.m. Probably time I go start to get ready for my date.

I get up and wash my dishes first before heading in to take a shower. Letting the warmth of the hot water soak in, just enjoying the calm it brings. I get out of the shower and just throw on a pair of shorts and a singlet while I look for something to wear on the date. Then I hear the door buzzer.

One of the guards comes over the intercom. 'Sorry for the intrusion, ma'am. We have just received a delivery for you. Would you like one of us to bring it up to your apartment?'

Delivery, what delivery? 'Yes, please bring it up.'

A few moments go by and there is a knock at my door. Through the electronic view panel on the door I see the guard, as expected. I open the door and they hand me a midsized box. It's not very heavy but of reasonable size.

'Thank you.'

He nods and I close the door. I walk through into my bedroom placing the box on the bed and open the lid. It's clothes. Shoes, underwear and a beautiful, figure-hugging mini dress. It's a little on the shorter side but it's the right size.

'Foresight, I hope you don't mind but I took the liberty of getting you a new outfit for tonight's date. Do you like them?'

Wow, Sarina is behind this.

I smile. 'Why did you think I needed a new outfit?' I pull the outfit out of the box laying the clothes on the bed. They are beautiful, she chose well. I don't know how I am going to look but I love them. 'I have learned that when a girl likes a boy, like you like Shadow, they sometimes get dressed up to impress their potential mate.'

Potential mate. Wow, slow down, Sarina.

'Yes, girls and boys do sometimes get a little dressed up when they go on a date with someone they have feelings for. Yes, I have some feelings for Shadow, but potential mate? I don't know about any of that. But yes, you chose well. Thank you for the dress.'

Her avatar appears on the TV in my room and she smiles at me. I still haven't gotten used to that.

'You're welcome.'

I change into the new underwear and dress. The dress is very figure-hugging; it's a good thing I'm in the best shape of my life.

'Wait, hang on, Sarina. How did you pay for this?'

She straightens up and the smile fades. 'I used the Vulcan funds, nothing extravagant.' Well, at least she didn't hack the store or something. We are supposed to be the good guys after all. This is definitely the better option.

'That's fine.'

I need to do something with my hair and decide that I will just make it look nice and leave it out. I run my fingers through it, scrunching it slightly in my hands to help form up the curls. After a few minutes of perfecting, I am finally happy with how it looks. I slide on the new heels that match the dress and walk over to the mirror. I almost don't believe my eyes. I look really hot. This dress is perfect for me, it hugs me in all the right places and really complements my body. Shadow is going to love this outfit. *I* love this outfit.

I'm looking my best for the date, so I really hope Shadow does a little better than jeans and a t-shirt or I'll be way overdressed.

I look up at the clock and it is a few minutes to seven. Time to head downstairs to meet up with Shadow. I take one more look in the mirror. *Looking good, Sam. Looking real good.* I walk into the kitchen and pick up my phone and a small handbag before I head downstairs. I have butterflies in my stomach. The elevator stops on the ground floor and the doors slowly open. As they do, I can see Shadow standing about halfway across the foyer, talking to one of the guards. When he sees me he stops midsentence. I step out of the elevator and start to walk towards them.

Shadow looks over to the guard and says something to him quickly, and the guard nods before walking back over towards the guard desk. He nods slightly as he passes me. I look back at Shadow and he hasn't taken his eyes off me. By the looks, Sarina has helped him out with his outfit as well; he's dressed in a nice shirt and suit. No tie, but he looks really good. I stop in front of him. He looks up to the camera and nods at the camera. I assume he approves of Sarina's choice.

'You look amazing,' he says.

I smile. 'You don't look so bad yourself. I think we can both thank our fairy godmother for the amazing outfits. She has great taste, I have to give her that.'

He smiles at me, running his eyes over my outfit, making me feel a little self-conscious.

'She certainly does, but I think it's you who makes that dress look good, not the other way around.' I fight back a blush. His words give me a little confidence boost. I take a breath, calming my nerves.

'So where are we going?'

He smiles. 'I've booked us a table at a restaurant overlooking the water and city lights. Sarina, can you bring around the car?' He gestures for us to head out the front and I do. He walks alongside me, never taking his eyes off me.

'What? Why are you staring at me?'

He shrugs almost awkwardly. 'Sorry, you just look so amazing, I can't help but look.'

We reach the doors and he gestures for me to walk through. He continues to watch me as we walk towards the car. When we arrive, he opens the door for me and I get in. He gently closes the door and walks around the driver's side to get in.

He lets Sarina do the driving and we talk about everything that has happened over the last week, particularly Vulcan's first mission. Shadow doesn't like the attention the press conference could have on us even though we were officially kept out of it. I agree it could bring unwanted scrutiny on an already precarious situation. We need to stay hidden, like we don't exist.

When we arrive, an attendant opens my door, helping me out of the vehicle. I am careful as I exit the vehicle – the dress is very short, and the heels are quite high. I'm trying my best to appear as I belong in these clothes. The valet takes the keys for the car and opens the door for us to enter the restaurant. Sarina could park the car herself, but we all play along, even Sarina; we don't like to reveal her presence unless necessary.

As we walk through the door we are greeted by an usher. 'Good evening, do you have a reservation this evening?'

Shadow steps forward. 'Yes, we have a reservation under Michael Knight.'

I have to stop myself from laughing. Really, Shadow, Michael Knight? Knight Rider and KITT. I guess it's fitting. Knight Rider was a favourite of my dad's, he loved the idea of a self driving car who could talk. We do have a talking, self-driving car. Not named KITT but it is still very fitting. I'm not surprised he didn't use his actual name but I didn't expect him to have a sense of humour doing it.

The usher gestures for us to follow him. Shadow takes my hand. As soon as he does, I get a tingling sensation all over, starting from the points where our skin touches. An electric surge rushes through my body. It's exhilarating. Shadow pulls me gently forward after the usher, walking through the restaurant to an elevator at the back of the room. They press the button and the doors open. They hold the door open and gestured for us to enter. We do, and the usher enters after us and turns to face to the doors as they close, taking us up. The doors open to a room overlooking the full nightscape, beautiful city lights, and the distant glimmer of the ocean in the distance, visible under the moonlight.

We are led across the room to a single table, set up for two. I look around the area. We are alone, this is all for us. Wow, Shadow has gone to a bit of effort with this, this is next level. I have to admit, I'm a little impressed. A waiter enters from one side and pulls out my chair for me. I sit and they slide the chair back in under me. Shadow sits opposite me on the table.

'I will leave you both now in the capable hands of your waiter,

Winston. He will ensure you have everything you need for the remainder of your evening,' the usher says before departing, gesturing to the man who helped me to my seat.

The waiter brings us a bottle of sweet white wine, pouring us a glass each. Shadow and I pick up our glasses, taking a sip. It is a spectacular location. He has certainly set the bar high for our first real date, if you don't count the hacker's duel or the movie night in the bunker. We talk and slowly enjoy our first glass. As we finish, Winston returns. 'Are you both ready to start entrées?' Shadow nods and they disappear bringing back our first dish. I'm not sure what it is but it looks fancy. He returns a few minutes later, refilling our drinks.

We continue our way through the dishes, never being asked for what we want. Shadow must have prearranged everything. He thought this all through: great location, preordered food of stuff I actually like. This is definitely the best date ever. Although I shouldn't be surprised, Shadow is a details kind of guy. It's hard not to be impressed.

After all the courses are complete and we have had a little more wine, I see Shadow signal the waiter. Are we done or is there more to come? Then I hear it, a small classical band, violins and flute. It is beautiful. He slides his chair back.

Oh crap. He wants to dance. Dancing is not something I am good at.

My suspicion is confirmed when he puts out his hand for me to take. 'May I have this dance?'

I look him in the eyes, I can't help but give in. I take his hand and we make our way a little further out into a balcony space. There is a light breeze carrying with it a hint of the distant ocean. He pulls me close, pressing our bodies together.

He leads me through the dance, guiding my every move. We flow together, gently dancing, around the balcony. The moment is intoxicating. My whole being is alive with excitement. It's like we are alone in the world, just the two of us gliding around, becoming one with the music.

I don't know how long we dance. It felt like only minutes but I know it's much longer. The city has become much quieter. When we finally stop, we walk over to the edge of the balcony, taking in the sights. It is a little chilly. I start to get goosebumps spreading across my body. Shadow must notice and puts his jacket around me, pulling me close again to help keep me warm. I turn to look at him. This has been a magical night, one I will not forget. He looks down into my eyes, smiling at me.

'How did I do?'

I smile. He did great. To answer his question, I lean in and kiss him gently, feeling the intoxicating rush of electricity through my body as I do. It takes my breath away. A brilliant end to a truly special night.

CHAPTER 29

BLURRED LINES

I wake to the smell of coffee brewing in my kitchen. I'm still a little foggy from sleep. It was a late night last night and the date with Shadow was amazing. We drank, we ate, we danced, and we kissed. At the thought of it, I can almost feel his body pressing against mine, the taste of the sweet wine on his lips. A night I will not forget in a while. Is that where it ended though? Why can I smell coffee? We drank a bit last night, did it go further? I look down and my dress is gone. I'm sleeping in just my underwear.

Is Shadow here or is it just me?

'Sarina, is anyone else in my apartment?'

Her image comes up on the TV on the other side of my room. 'No, Foresight, you are alone in the apartment. Shadow escorted you to your room and after a few extended moments in the elevator left to return to his apartment around 2 a.m.'

Okay, so we got a little heavy but nothing too crazy. That's good to know.

As the fog of sleep starts to clear, I start to remember the final moments of my night. The pure ecstasy, the rush, the hunger. It was hard to resist, but we did. We respected each other and left it a perfect night.

'Sarina, why is there a smell of coffee in my room then?'

'I am brewing it for you with your machine in the kitchen. I believe that a nice cup of coffee after a big night can help get you firing on all cylinders, so to speak.' She is right, I could really do with a cup of coffee. 'Did you enjoy your date with Shadow last night?'

A smile creeps across my face. I couldn't hide it if I wanted to. 'Last night was great. I had a wonderful time with Shadow. I am hoping we can do it again soon.' She smiles, she seems pleased by the news.

Shower time. I need to get rid of any of that leftover fog from sleep. I have to finish my report on our team's last operation – the prime minister would like to know the complete details of what went down.

I have a quick shower and get ready for work, enjoying a cup of that coffee on the balcony before I make my way down to the lair. I gather up my things, refilling my cup before heading down.

As I walk through the doors into the lair, I can see the whole team in their seats, collating and putting together their parts of the report. I chose well with this lot. They really do want to be here. I sit down at my desk looking over at Shadow as I do.

He smiles. 'Good morning, Foresight.'

I smile back. 'Good morning, Shadow.'

The others are looking at us; they know something is going on. But it's not like we've we hidden our feelings from anyone. We just aren't saying anything either.

The team won't say anything unless we bring it up – we are all very private people. That's just the nature of who we all are. Hackers. We all just get to work, everyone doing what they need to do, even Shadow.

After a few hours, I have everyone's section of the report I need and I dismiss them all, telling them to enjoy the downtime while they have a chance because we never know what will come up next. Shadow hangs back as he usually does, waiting to see me alone. When Hammer, the last of the other members, leaves, Shadow gets up, walks over next to me and sits down on my desk. I look up at him. 'I hope you had a good night last night, boss.'

I try to hold a poker face, not showing any reaction, any feelings either way about the situation. 'Yeah, it was okay.' He looks at me almost disappointedly, but I can't hold it in any longer. I laugh. 'Of course I did, silly. It was a great night. Thank you for all the effort you put in to make it so special.'

He softens now, taking a deep breath. He thought I was serious for a moment. 'That's good. I was worried there for a moment.'

He reaches out, touching the side of my face, gently moving his fingers down across my cheek, tracing part of my cheekbone and jawline before continuing down my neck towards my shoulders. His touch excites me; I don't want him to stop. I focus, take a breath, calming my nerves. I need to talk to him about some boundaries. It needs to be now, before things get too deep. If he doesn't want boundaries, we will need to end it now before it gets too serious, before it can affect the team.

'Shadow, we need to talk.'

The smile on his face fades and he stops touching me. I said the dreaded words no one wants to hear when in a relationship, especially if you aren't sure where you stand. He gets off my desk and sits on his chair, wheeling it closer so we can sit face to face. He looks a little worried. Maybe he thinks I am unsure we should continue this. Maybe he thinks this is a 'We should just be friends' talk.

'Last night was great – I had an amazing time. There is certainly something strong between us, I can feel it and I think you can too.' I fidget in my chair a little before continuing. 'I want to set some rules for our relationship if it's going to continue, ones to protect us and our team moving forward. These are a must.'

He's watching me, trying to figure out what is going through my mind. He has what can only be considered a poker face, careful not to reveal his reaction to what I am saying.

We look at each other for a moment before I continue.

'I like you. I want you to know that first.' He must be concerned about where this is going because he stiffens slightly in his chair. 'I am worried about how our relationship will change the dynamics of Vulcan. If we are not careful, we could cause permanent damage to the group, and if Vulcan fails, it could have dire consequences for both Hammer and yourself. I don't want either of you to go back to jail. I'll try to protect you both no matter what happens between us, but the risk still exists.'

I can see Shadow prepare to respond, to pitch his argument, I assume, for our relationship, but I put up my hand stopping him. 'This is not the "I just want to be friends" talk. That's not what I want at all. I do need to protect the team from us though. That needs to be a priority.'

He nods. 'I agree. We need to ensure this does not come back on the team if it doesn't work out between us. I understand that. Boundaries, you said. What boundaries?'

'Firstly, we need to keep us, whatever that ends up being, completely separate from our work. No affection, no touching and no personal interaction of any kind during work scenarios. We need to be one hundred per cent professional the whole time we are doing anything to do with work. I'm not saying we need to hide it, I want to do the opposite actually. I want to tell the rest of the team that we are going to be dating.'

He seems to be thinking about what I said. 'So, what I just did, touching your face, physical affection is off-limits but only while we are in the lair or doing work-related activities? Outside of that we are free to pursue all activities?' He grins at me on that last point. He is being a little cheeky with me. I ignore it for now. I need to make sure he understands this is serious, this needs to happen in order to make our relationship a possibility.

'No PDA of any type during work-related activities. I need you to agree and understand this. This is how I need it to be. I can't risk our team over this, the work we will do is too important. Are you on board with this? Or do we need to stop this now before it gets any more complicated?'

He straightens up again, all seriousness back in his appearance and voice. 'I am on board with whatever you need to allow us to pursue… us. I want to find out what we could be. I know it has some risks and I agree we need to be careful not to make this a problem for the team if it doesn't turn out the way we both want it to go. Sometimes things just don't work out. I'm hoping we don't end up that way but we need to ensure that we have things in place to make this a safe space, to not cause any ripples in the team's fabric.' He reaches out to take my hands, looking me in the eyes.

'You have my word, I will stick to your boundaries. It won't be easy, not being able to touch you, to kiss those lips of yours, but I will keep the boundaries. We are worth the effort, the challenges that this will bring, I know we are.'

I'm relieved. This has gone much better than I thought. We are both of the same opinion: we need to protect the team from ourselves. What we have in Vulcan is important, we can make a real difference in our world. Our relationship can not be allowed to put that at risk.

We seem to both relax a little, I am enjoying the touch of his hands holding mine. I'm still nervous about where this relationship will go but I know we are worth it, Shadow is worth it. Now that conversation has been had, we both know what page the other is on. He smiles at me and just sits there looking at me for a moment.

'So, when can we see each other again in a personal sense?'

I smile, thinking back to our date. 'Soon. I need to work tonight,

I must take the report to the prime minister personally this afternoon – I will be trying out our new helicopter. It arrived this morning with the new vehicles.'

He nods. 'Do you need company?'

I consider it for a moment. No, I don't think I do. I should do this one alone. It will give less coverage to the other members of my team. I need to make sure I keep them safe and that means being the face of the group, keeping the other members hidden for their own safety. Part of being their leader is ensuring I shield them from external influences. 'Thanks, but I can handle this one. Have some fun, go out with the team or something. I think you all need to blow off a bit of steam.'

CHAPTER 30

MEETING ON THE HILL

I climb into the new helicopter on the roof of our building. This is going to come in handy, having a company helicopter that is, especially such an advanced piece of gear. It is fully loaded with weapons but also has enough tech in it to allow Sarina to truly make this a very capable addition to our team. Plus, it will let me fly to the capital in under an hour instead of driving for over ten hours for a meeting. A much better option even if technically I wouldn't be driving, Sarina would, but that's not the point.

I start to clip myself in when the doors start to close.

'Foresight, are you ready to go?' Sarina asks. 'We have the all-clear to take off. Our flight plan has been lodged. I will also reactivate the tracking system once we are out of the city to ensure our rides benefactors don't have our lair's location.'

'Yes, let's head out. Why don't we see what this thing is capable of?'

The engines start and the blades kick into high gear. It only takes a few seconds before we are in the air and hurtling towards our destination. I don't know how fast this thing can go, but it is certainly quick, that I know for sure. I am not sure I will need an hour to get to Canberra if we can keep this pace up. I watch the ground pass under us like a blur. Sarina is keeping us fairly low, under the radar floor for the first fifteen minutes of our trip, before climbing to a more normal height as we approach the range, switching on our tracking systems.

After about forty minutes, we're heading towards a largely populated area. But we couldn't be in Canberra yet, could we?

'Foresight, we are approaching the destination. Two air force helicopters are tracking towards our location fast and I have provided our clearance details. We have been approved for landing on the hill but will be escorted into the airspace. Do you want me to slow our pace so they can keep up?'

I smile. At this pace, they have no chance of staying with us.

'Nah, let them try to catch us.'

As we approach the lodge, the prime minister's residence, I hear warning bells go off.

'Sarina, what is that?' I look around the dashboards, trying to see for myself.

'They have a lock on us from the facility's weapons systems. There are four different trackers locked on us and the helicopters have now finally caught up to us as well.' I didn't know that they had missile defence systems at the lodge. I wonder what else the rest of the world doesn't know either.

'Could we survive a strike if we are targeted?'

I don't get an immediate response, I assume she is considering all options. 'The likelihood of attack is very low, Foresight, but if they chose to strike, and with the advanced capabilities of our ride, we would have more than seventy per cent chance of survival unscathed. It's hard to get exact statistics with the number of unknowns we have in this situation. The success would be high though, I feel. Do you plan on attacking the location? If so, I will prepare for a quick exit.'

I smile. 'No, I have no plans on escalating this into a conflict, but it doesn't hurt to know our surroundings and have an exit strategy if things go south quickly. Just a habit, I guess, and good practice for future situations that may not be so friendly.' I think I will always look at scenarios like this – it is just how I am wired now. I can't help but look at things, analyse every angle, make sure I have a way out if needed.

'I will expand my knowledge on the capabilities of the site while you are in your meeting, so I can generate an exit strategy in case we need it.'

We start to descend onto the helipad. I can see the grounds guards watching us from all angles and the helicopters hovering above us ready to react if I am deemed to be a threat. I guess I should see it as a compliment that they see us as a threat. You can't blame them, really. My team did just destroy an army to the west and rescue the prime minister. That kind of makes us a high-risk opponent if we decided to turn on them. We are still a very unknown commodity, a secret black ops team that no one even knew existed who just showed up and saved the day before dropping off the face of the earth again until about twenty minutes ago when our ride dropped back onto the radar.

The attack on the prime minister's convoy and his kidnapping could be the cause of the security escalation. They would certainly not want something like that happening again. Nothing like that has ever happened in Australia. We have always just been that little brother helping out our bigger allies UK and US in conflicts, making them the primary targets in most instances, but we should have seen this coming, been more prepared with the increase in our participation in bringing down terrorist regimes or fighting injustice with dictatorships. I am surprised we have not had any other attacks before now.

Going after the prime minister is a bold move, but they could have gone on a shooting spree, blown something up or done a number of things. The engines on the helicopter start to wind down, so I unbuckle myself and grab my bag.

I climb out and am instantly greeted by two of the guards, 'Identification, please,' one of them says.

I pull out my ASD identification. He scans my ID, bringing up my information on his tablet – I can see on the screen it marks my details as classified. It almost completely redacted except for my name, my position as a black ops operative and the note giving full access clearance.

The guard looks up at me. 'Ma'am, please follow me. He is waiting for you.'

The two guards turn and head towards the building in front of me, with two more guards falling in behind me. They lead me through the residence to what looks to be a sitting room. The prime minister sits on one of the chairs in front of an open fire. As soon as he sees me, he rises from his chair and puts his hand out for me to shake. I take it, shaking it firmly, looking him directly in the eyes as I do.

'I am glad you could make the trip to bring me this report, Sam. I wanted to have the opportunity to thank you for what you and your team did for me. Thanks to your team, my wife and kids still have a father, and our country still has their prime minister. I am personally very thankful for what you did, getting me out in one piece. And from what I am told you stopped not only another set of attacks in our country but helped our US counterparts to remove a similar threat in their country before it got too far advanced. That assistance will not go forgotten, something that will truly help our country's ties in the future.'

'Just doing our job, sir. We were ecstatic that we were able to get you out in time, safe and unharmed. I will personally pass on your thanks to my team. Considering what we do daily, as you can imagine, I can't reveal their identities for their and their families' safety.'

He nods, gesturing for me to take a seat as he returns to his own. 'So you and your team are completely black ops, no formal ties to our government and complete autonomy. Do I have that right?' I nod and he continues. 'I am told your team is still relatively new, but you have already done things no one before you has ever been able to do. I have to say, I am impressed. Not just about my rescue and the precision that was carried out but by how your team can achieve such results in such a short time.'

'Thank you, sir. You are correct: we are still a new team but the team has integrated very well and we work well as one.' I am starting to wonder what this is about. Why am I really here? Does he want something from us or did he just want to shake my hand, meet someone from the team who saved his life? No point beating around the bush, I might as well just ask and get it out of the way. 'Is there a reason you wanted to see me, sir? Not that I'm not enjoying our conversation. I'm stoked to meet with the prime minister of my country. It just feels like you want something from Vulcan? Do you?'

He turns in his chair slightly. 'Yes, I do have two reasons for asking you to meet with me today. The first was just to thank you and the other is to ask you to do something for me. There is a state-sponsored criminal group that has been targeting a lot of critical infrastructure of late, not just in Australia but other allies as well. I want your team to find them and... How shall I put this? Show them that attacking us would not be in their best interests. Your group can do this without any specific backlash on our government, but the criminals will understand the message nonetheless.'

He picks up a folder with what looks to be about ten to fifteen pages in it. Not a very thorough dossier, but I guess it's something. He hands it to me and I open it to take a quick look over the contents. 'I know as an independent group you have no formal requirements to follow my orders or direction, but will you do it?'

I flick through a few more of the pages and lift my head to look him in the eyes. 'Sir, Vulcan will take care of this, but I want to be very clear with you on something, just so we are on the same page. Vulcan will not be a personal attack dog for the government. We are here to stop the worst of the worst and we will not defer from our mission to make the world a better place. That is our mission. If it is deemed that this group is not a priority, it will be pushed back. Is that acceptable to you?'

He looks a little surprised by my statement. He probably isn't used to people saying no to him or maybe it's the fact that I am so young and a girl. It takes guts I guess to basically just school the PM without a care in the world. Cool as a cucumber, as Dad would say, or maybe just stupid. If I am honest with myself, it's probably a little of both.

The prime minister seems to come to terms with it quickly, recovering his composure and relaxes in his chair. 'I was told you wouldn't blindly take orders, that you are one of true conviction. I am not sure if I could be more impressed with you. Your team can always count on my support. I know you have to keep in the shadows to an extent, but if you find yourselves in a situation that you need support, I will take your call any time of day.'

'Thank you, sir. I appreciate your support and your understanding of my team's true purpose. I will ensure you receive an update on the outcome of your request.' He nods and I continue. 'Sir–'

He puts his hand up. 'You saved my life. I am certain you have earned the right to drop the formalities and speak candidly with me. By the look on your face, you want to ask me something I may not like.' I nod. 'Continue.'

'Before you were attacked and taken hostage, who knew the direct route your convoy would take? Is it a regular path or do you change it up constantly? I just have concerns as to how they knew you would be in that location at that time.'

He looks a little taken back by the statement, as though he had just eaten something sour. 'Why do you ask? Do you feel this could be an inside job?'

I look him straight in the eyes. 'I don't know. It's why I want to know if this was a known route or something that someone would have had to know. The terrorists didn't have access to the camera network. We did, a few minutes after your attack. No satellite support to track your convoy and I didn't see anything to indicate your vehicles had any tracking devices.'

He shifts in his chair a little. I can see he is thinking about it. 'I know you wouldn't want to believe it was one of your team, but if there is a possibility, I want to look into it further. I needed to pull the nagging thread, get an answer so that if it is nothing I can let it go.'

He nods. 'I believe we used the same path the morning before I was attacked. Maybe they were watching and knew we used the same path on both trips to and from the location. I don't think the route would be common knowledge and now you have said it, I don't know.'

'Your theory could be right. Maybe you were followed that morning and they just gambled on you taking the same reverse journey. I will look into it and confirm our theory though before I put it to rest. If someone followed you, we will find evidence of such.' He looks happier that I am going to look into it. I think if it was me, I would want to know.

'In the meantime, watch your back just in case my hunch has some grounding to it and you have someone in your team that doesn't have your best interests at heart.' He nods and I stand, extending my hand towards him. I think I surprised him again. Maybe he doesn't normally get told when a meeting is done. I assume he is the one who normally makes that call.

'Thank you again for your assistance. I will await your update. Call me anytime. As I said, I will take your call.' He shakes my hand and I turn to walk out when he says one last comment. 'I think our country is very lucky to have you and your team on our side. Thank you again.' I just nod and smile before continuing to exit the room.

As I walk out of the room and close the door behind me, two guards, one from either side, approach me.

'This way back to your ride, ma'am.'

I follow them, weaving back through the way I had come. It's a nice place, old and not quite my style, but a beautiful house nonetheless. I can only imagine the stories these walls could tell from over the years, the under-table deals or arguments or even the scandal. It would certainly be interesting, that's for sure.

We reach the outer door leading back to the chopper and I see one of the guards peering through the window.

'Can I help you?' I say. He jumps, I seem to have surprised him.

'Sorry, ma'am, I was going to check out your ride for threats as per normal procedure but it has no handles. It seems to be locked and when I touched the side, it warned me I would regret it the next time I laid a hand on the vehicle.'

I smile. It sounds like Sarina was having some fun while I was talking with the PM. He looks at me for a moment. 'What is this thing? I've never seen anything like it. Who the hell are you?'

I smile at him. 'We are not of your concern and you have never seen me or this machine behind you. It is better for you that way, if you forget us.'

His expression quickly straightens, like he has been caught with his hand in the cookie jar. 'Ma'am, yes, ma'am.'

All of the guards straighten up and stood to attention.

'Sarina, let's get out of here,' I say quietly, so the guards don't overhear. The side opens up, allowing me access. I look over at the guard's face and he can't hide his astonishment. He sees me look at him and closes his gaping mouth.

I climb in and within a few seconds, we are off the ground and heading back home. I probably shouldn't have had fun with the poor guy. What he matters doesn't really think, but he probably thinks I am in some super-secret hit squad or something, a super-spy. Like James Bond, but cooler. I'm not just the love interest – I'm a badass chick.

CHAPTER 31

BREAKING THE RULES

The afternoon started out pretty uneventful; I got back to the building and headed back to my apartment, had some lunch and just relaxed on the couch for a while until Shadow texted me: *Deano and his team are in Brisbane. He wanted to know if we wanted to meet him tonight, to get to know each other better, to share a drink and maybe if it all goes well, discuss what you wanted to discuss with him?*

It sounds like an invite, for both Shadow and me, which makes sense – Deano has had a long-term relationship with Shadow. However, Deano and I are still just getting to know each other.

Where did he want to meet? I text back. I hope it's somewhere nice. I like the idea of getting a little dressed up again and spending some more time with Shadow. But I'll need to be careful, this will be work-related and I need to not cross a boundary.

A whiskey bar in the Valley, just a short drive from the lair.

That sounds fine, a bit more casual but still upmarket enough to make sure I look good, enough to raise Shadow's heart rate a little.

Let him know we are in, we will meet him at eight.

A nice, relaxing night out will do me good. 'Sarina, you don't happen to have any more outfits up your sleeves, do you? Something I will look killer in for a whiskey bar?'

Her avatar pops up on the TV in front of me. 'I have the perfect thing. It will be delivered within the hour.'

'Wow, thank you, you're a lifesaver. It's not too dressy though, is it?'

She smiles at me. 'It will be perfect. I will get the vehicles ready for use. Will we need air support with the Vulcan copter or any Loyal Wingmen?'

Wow, she is ready to rumble. Maybe she thinks I am a magnet for trouble and need to be prepared for anything. I did say she should be prepared for all outcomes. 'Have the helicopter on standby, but no need to be brought out unless needed. Ensure the vehicles are ready to go and bring two escort vehicles, just in case.'

'Understood. I will prep the convoy and generate a full contingency plan in the event of an incident. Also, your outfit is now on its way and will be delivered in approximately thirty minutes. The desk has been informed of the delivery and will bring it up as soon as it arrives.

'Thank you, Sarina.' I can see why Shadow had put so much effort into making Sarina a reality. It's great having Sarina around to help get things organised. But I think her creation also may have had a little to do with him being alone, giving him someone to talk to.

I feel for him, knowing what he has been through. It would have been hard being alone, dealing with what happened to his family.

He never trusted anyone in his life. It was all an act to keep his real-world a secret. I know how that feels. It's hard hiding your real self from the world, not having someone that you can share your complete self with. This team is different; it lets us be our true selves. There's no hiding we are who we are – for better or worse our complete selves are on the table for all to see. Well, mostly. Every one of us still has some secrets but we don't need to hide, that's what matters, we can belong without judgement or repercussions.

Shadow and I are a little more complicated. We are similar creatures. We thrive in the hacker world; we are much more than that though, we sync like we were made for each other. Like Shadow was programmed to be my ying and I programmed to be his yang. It's hard to explain but the chemistry, the skills, all complement each other.

BZZZZ. The buzzer interrupts my thoughts. Oh, it'll be my outfit. What did Sarina get me?

I head to the door, checking who it is before opening the door for the guard.

'I have a delivery for you, ma'am. Sarina, your assistant, told us it would be arriving and to bring it right up.'

Assistant, hey? That's the perfect cover. They just think Sarina is my assistant, not a super-intelligent AI entity living out of a super-secret quantum computing system hidden in the just as super-secret hidden black ops base five stories or more under the parking garage. I smile. If only people knew the whole truth.

'Thank you, I appreciate you bringing it up for me.'

He smiles back, handing me the box. 'No problem at all, ma'am. If you need anything else at all just let me know.' He lingers for a moment then awkwardly smiles and leaves. I have the weird feeling he wants to ask me something, but wasn't quite brave enough.

I call after him, 'Did you want something else? It seemed like you were about to say something.'

He stops in his tracks and turns to look at me, starting to go a little red around his cheeks.

'Yes, I wanted to say that, umm, well, I–'

Crap. I should have left it be. This is awkward. 'I think you're beautiful, ma'am. I wanted to ask you out on a date, sometime, if you were so inclined.'

I smile – looks like Shadow has some competition. Sadly for this guy, I don't think anyone could hold a candle to Shadow or even be in the same league.

'Oh. Thank you. But I'm actually seeing someone at the moment.' The guard looks at his feet, fidgeting a little. 'I appreciate the gesture though and your very kind words.'

He smiles at me. 'You're welcome. Sorry for even mentioning it, ma'am. I know it's inappropriate but it was worth a shot.'

I nod. 'It was definitely worth a shot.'

He nods and takes his leave and I close the door to my apartment, sagging against the door. Well, that certainly got a little uncomfortable.

I take the clothes into the bedroom, sit the box down on the bed and open it up to take a look at the outfit Sarina has chosen for me. It's a blue dress. It's going to be quite figure-hugging. A little more on the casual side than the last one, but still dressy enough. It's a little longer too, but still way above my knee. There are also a set of high heels with a blue see-through lace-like material that covers the entire foot, zippers up the back that all extends a few inches above the ankle. They are beautiful.

This outfit is definitely killer, that's for sure. I can see Sarina's avatar on the screen behind me, wearing a look of anticipation. 'Well, did I get it right? Do you like them?'

'I think we will have to wait and see how it looks on, but I think you did it again, Sarina. I think you nailed it. This is certainly going to get Shadow's heart racing.'

I still have some time before I need to get ready so I make myself a coffee and just chill out for a while. I have something to eat and then go for a shower. I take my time, in no rush to get ready. Once I am dressed, I look in the mirror, looking over the woman standing before me. I am not a young girl anymore, I am a confident, beautiful woman who happens to lead the most kickass black ops team in the country, maybe even the world. It's crazy how far I have come in such a short time.

Only a year ago, as I finished high school, I would have rolled around the floor laughing at anyone who would have suggested this is what I would be doing now. But that was before I decided to dive down the cyber spy rabbit hole. It's not a decision I regret. I would definitely take the red pill again, no question, but it certainly changed my life and the other members of my team. For the better, but still, it's a lot in just a short time.

'Well, Sarina, what do you think? Did you get it right?'

I can see her smile. 'Oh, I got it right. You look amazing.' I have to agree with her, I do look good.

'Sarina, please let Shadow know I will meet him outside the elevator in the car park. Have the cars waiting for me. It's time to get our very own assault team by bringing Deano and his team into the Vulcan fold.'

Her avatar disappears from the screen. I gather up my things – phone, wallet, coat – and head to the elevator. The doors open to the carpark and I can see Shadow waiting for me, leaning against the hood of the middle vehicle. He is dressed nicely, nothing over the top, but he looks good.

As I step out of the elevator, I can see him watching me. I can see the outfit is getting the desired response. Tick, heart rate elevated.

I smile as I get closer to him. 'Shadow.'

He smiles back. 'Foresight.'

He strolls over and opens my door for me. I slide in and he closes it behind me before walking around the other side. When he gets in and closes the door I can't help but give him a lingering glance. The familiar butterflies flutter to life in my stomach, something I am not sure I will ever get used to.

'Sarina, let's go.'

The convoy leaves the building, heading out through the city towards our destination. Shadow takes my hand and I let him, glancing over as he slides his fingers between my own. This is a work thing. I should stop him, but I don't.

When we arrive at the location, the two escort vehicles block the entrance while the valet opens my door for me. I slide out. Shadow exits the car from his side and makes his way around to me.

'Will you need your vehicles parked today?' the valet asks.

I turn to look at him. 'No, we will not need a parking service, the cars will return when we are ready to leave.'

He nods, closing the door behind me, before heading to open the door to the club. 'Enjoy your evening.'

I nod. 'Thank you, we will.'

Shadow and I make our way through the club, keeping an eye out for Deano and his team. They are at the back of the club, in the VIP section. He gestures for the guard on the entrance to allow us in and he opens the rope barrier as we approach. We head over to the lounge area where he is sitting with his team. He gets to his feet and hugs me like we have known each other for years. I embrace him back. He did save my life, so I think that makes him almost family. He releases me and does the same to Shadow but maybe a little more aggressive and playful as they slap each other on the back.

After a few moments, Deano gestures for us to sit. We do and he orders us a round of drinks. We talk and laugh for what feels like hours. It's a great night – Deano and his team are fun to be around, I don't think I have had this much fun in so long. It's good to just relax. Before I know it, the evening is getting late and I still haven't recruited him.

'Deano, we need to talk about some more serious things.'

He looks at me. 'Talk can wait, we have fun now.'

I don't want to let it go but pushing it will not help me. So I just nod and just enjoy the rest of the night.

Shadow asks me to dance and we get a little heated on the dance floor. We're almost in our own world, leaving everything and everyone behind for a few minutes. I shouldn't have allowed it to go this far, I should have refused the offer to dance, but we are having such a good night, I just wanted to enjoy the moment. I look him in the eyes, losing myself in them.

'Foresight, apologies for interrupting your dance but we seem to have company. There are a couple of goons in a car outside the club that pulled up about twenty minutes ago. I don't know who they are here for, but you should exit and so should Deano's team. If they need an exit vehicle, I will bring the second vehicle in for pickup.'

I snap back to reality, switching instantly back into focus. I stop dancing, whispering in Shadow's ear, 'It's time to go.' I take his hand and head over to Deano. I lean over, whispering in his ear, 'We have some company outside, I don't know if they are here for any of us but it's time to go.'

He barks a single command to his men and they snap back to focus, all seeming to instantly sober up. They form a defensive pattern around us, watching all angles for a threat.

'Do you need a ride out of here?' I ask.

Deano shakes his head. 'We have a vehicle waiting out back.'

I nod. 'We'll head out the front and clear the way for your exit.'

He nods and his team moves.

Shadow and I make our way towards the front. 'Sarina, we are on our way out. Get things ready for a quick pickup.'

As we approach the doors, I can see our vehicles block the driveway as they did on drop off, but this time Sarina angles the car into the doorway, covering us as we exit. As we approach she opens the door and I slide in, Shadow quickly following me. The valet attendant looks a little surprised by what is happening but we doesn't say anything.

Our convoy leaves quickly in a defensive formation. We make our way out of the city.

'Sarina, are we being followed?'

'Initially, yes, they had started to follow us, but we have been able to lose them. We are clear. I am also tracking Deano. His team was able to slip away. It would seem we were the target, not Deano.' That's good to know. 'I will take the long way back to the building just to ensure we are all clear.'

I wonder who it was; why they were following us. Maybe it's one of the agencies trying to find out more information about us or someone one of the team has pissed off at some point. That list seems to be growing every day. The thought makes me smile. What a life.

I relax a little, more comfortable with our situation. The adrenaline is still pumping strong but at least now there is no immediate threat.

I look over at Shadow, remembering our dance. It had been such a nice night. He stares straight into my eyes before leaning in a little closer. 'I enjoyed tonight, I wish it wasn't ending so soon.' I have to agree with him, I don't want the night to end either. I lean in a little closer, kissing Shadow with a little more passion than initially intended. He responds returning my passion.

I feel Shadow's hand on my thigh, sliding slowly higher up my leg. It almost makes my breath catch. What is he doing? I stop kissing him for a moment and he smiles, leaning in to kiss me again. My body ignites with his every touch. His hand brushes the outside of my knickers and I gasp at his touch. This is breaking the rules. We are not supposed to be doing any of this tonight. He doesn't move his hand any further, just leaves it there. He continues to kiss me, and my heart rate climbs. I feel like I am going to explode.

I am starting to lose control. I want him. I want him now. Twisting around to face him, I pull my dress up slightly so I can climb onto his lap, straddling him. I pull him closer, kissing him again. My hands are running over his chest and his heart pounds fast. His hands slide around behind me, pulling me to him, caressing my back. My every nerve is ignited, electrified. I let out a slight moan, pure enjoyment escaping into the world. He seems to respond to my release, sliding his hands up under my dress, igniting my senses even more, though I don't know how that is even possible.

We arrive at the building but I continue kissing him for a few moments, slowly climbing off his lap. I fix my dress as I do. I slide over, grabbing the handle and opening the door. The fresh air clears my mind and I climb out of the vehicle. Shadow quickly follows, fixing his clothes as he does. He looks a little hot under the collar.

I turn back and take his hand, walking towards the elevator. I press the up button and after a few moments, the doors open. We don't say anything while we wait for the elevator, just steal the occasional glance at each other. We enter the elevator.

Shadow turns to me. 'I had a great night tonight. I hope you did as well.'

He is saying good night. What? After that? He lifts his hand and selects my floor and then goes to click on his, but I touch his wrist and stop him.

'I think you should stay with me tonight.'

CHAPTER 32

THE MORNING AFTER

I wake to the smell of brewing coffee. It's a gentle smell on the air, just enough to encourage me to start to open my eyes. This all seems familiar, déjà vu, like it's all happened before. Am I still dreaming? I reach up and move my hair out of my face. The blinds are still closed, it's quite dark in here, I wonder what time it is.

'Sarina, open the blinds please.'

The blinds slowly move up and as my eyes adjust to the influx of light, I realise I'm naked, covered partially by the silk sheet draped over my body. I feel amazing, like I have had the best night's sleep ever. I stretch out slightly and touch something with my leg. Hang on. I roll over to see Shadow asleep next to me. He's also very naked but not as covered as me. I allow my eyes to linger over his naked body. Last night was amazing. More than I could have imagined. Not just the sex, yes, that was great, but the connection between us was truly electrifying.

He must sense me looking at him or perhaps the light has started to wake him. He opens his eyes, going through a similar realisation as I did.

After a few moments, looks me in the eyes. 'Good morning, Foresight.'

I smile at him, running my fingers down his chest, tracing his abs. 'Good morning, Shadow.'

We don't say anything more, just stare into each other's eyes, losing ourselves in the moment. After a few minutes, I lean forward, softly kissing him on the lips, feeling that same electricity rise at our very touch.

I pull back, smiling at him. 'I'm going to go grab a shower.' I turn to get out of the bed, letting the sheet fall away to reveal my naked body as I walk towards the bathroom. I can see him watching me. I stop as I reach the door. 'You're welcome to join me.'

Flashing a cheeky smile, I disappear through the door and start to turn on the shower. I let the water get to temperature and step under the water, closing my eyes, letting the water wash over me. Then I feel it, Shadow's hands around my waist, pulling me close to him, kissing me as the water washes over us.

The rest of the morning goes along slowly. We have coffee, breakfast and just hang out, talking about our families, our lives before Vulcan. It's a good day, a really good day.

'Foresight, you are needed in the bunker. Alone,' Sarina says.

Shadow looks at me. 'What's going on?'

I'm just as confused as he is. Why would Sarina want me in the bunker alone? What would require that level of secrecy?

'I don't know, but I will find out. Get ready to work, this might end up being a very long day.' I turn and start to head towards the secret elevator access when Shadow grabs my arm.

He stops me, pulling me back into him. 'Just in case I don't get to do this again today.' He kisses me with a little more passion than I expect, flooding me with adrenaline. My heart kicks into high gear, my cheeks flush. He steps back, smiling at me. 'I'll be waiting in my apartment for your every command, boss.'

I like that, maybe a little too much. I shake the desire to forget the world and spend the rest of the day in my bed with Shadow from my mind and turn to the access area. 'Sarina,' I say and she opens the access. I step into the waiting elevator. I make my way through the security doors and notice they close behind me sealing the access off, securing me inside.

'Foresight, I brought you here because we know this area is clean, no ears listening. I pulled on those strings, as you asked me too, on the prime minister's case. I think we have a problem, a rat inside his house. Someone with a lot of power.'

'Show me what you have found.' If this level of security is needed, they must be high up.

'It's the deputy prime minister. He accessed the information one hour before the attack on the secure convoy. He had also been accessing secure files I don't think he needs to. Something fishy is going on. Either his account has been hacked or he is a mole.'

If Sarina is right and he is the mole, we need to handle this with care. The evidence needs to be perfect. He's a powerful man in our country and if there is any doubt he will be able to walk away unscathed from this, whatever it is that he is trying to achieve by working with the terrorists. Was it out of a personal ambition to take the top job, to become prime minister? I hope he is just a victim of a security incident, and he isn't really behind this.

'Sarina, I need to see everything you have found. It's time to dig into the deputy's life, history, everything about him. Nothing can be left unturned. Also please tell Shadow I have something I need to take care of. I will find him later.'

I get to work, digging through everything I can find on the deputy, his emails, texts, I get access to everything. If there is a single crumb, a path that will lead us to the truth, I will not stop until we find it.

Sarina and I dig for hours. Nothing, not a thing that could link him to the terrorist group, no weird emails, texts, money, nothing at all. There has to be something.

'Sarina, I want you to track him, monitor his movements. I need to know everything that he does that seems out of the ordinary. Every small thing, no matter what it is. Okay.' I think it's time I take a break and think this over. 'I will be upstairs. I'm going to get something to eat.' I see the access doors start to open and I head out of the lair back up to my apartment.

I am missing something, the key to all of this, something big, I just don't know what it is yet.

CHAPTER 33

DEANO

I'm just sitting down and getting ready to eat when my phone vibrates with a text. It's Deano.

Do you want to have that talk now?

I need to talk to him. We could benefit from having his team become part of ours, to strike at the worlds worst and defend us when needed. They are the best at what they do; I don't want any other team. I trust him, he has earned that from me.

Yes. Where?

I watch the dots as he writes his reply.

What about the Pig and Whistle?

What the hell is a Pig and Whistle? I quickly google it on my phone – it's a restaurant in the city. *Sure, I will meet you there in an hour?*

I watch the dots scroll again. *Great, see you soon.*

I get up and take a look at my outfit in the mirror. It is semi-casual, just jeans and a nice shirt. I will grab a light jacket, that will work. I head into the cupboard and grab a black jacket off the coat hanger.

'Sarina, get a car ready for me, please. I'm heading out. No need for the escort this time, but have them at the ready in case.' I pull on the jacket and quickly brush my teeth.

'The car is waiting for you next to the elevator downstairs.'

I wipe my face and put on a quick spray of deodorant. Take another quick look in the mirror, good to go. I grab my bag off the shelf and head to the elevator. I go to press the button but before I do, the doors open. It's Shadow.

'Hey.' He smiles at me.

'Hey yourself.'

He steps out of the elevator and kisses me. I feel my breath catch slightly as he does. I am not sure I will ever get used to that. I kiss him back for a few moments before I pull back from his embrace.

'I am sorry, but I have to go.'

He looks at me for a moment. 'Do you need any help?' I shake my head.

'No, I am just going to talk with Deano. I want his team to join ours, work for me.' He seems a little unhappy with my answer.

'I figured that's what you wanted to talk to him about the other night. They would be a good addition. But they won't be cheap.' Shadow fidgets a little before continuing. 'You can lean on me you know, whatever you need. You don't need to be everything for everyone.'

I choose my words carefully. 'The best never are, but we need the best and I know I can.'

He smiles. 'Yes, we definitely do, don't we. With all the fights we're picking we will need them at some point, it's almost guaranteed. If I wanted anyone covering our backs it would be Deano's team, that's for sure.' He turns and presses the elevator button to bring it back to our floor. It opens and we both step in. He takes my hand as the doors close. I can feel the warmth of his skin on mine. It is just the smallest of contact between us but it has my heart pounding as though I have just run five kilometres. We get to the car park, and he walks me to the waiting car.

When we get to the car, he opens the door for me. He stops me before I get in.

'Let me know when you get back. I want to see you tonight, no matter what time.'

I smile and nod. He leans over, kissing me one more time, then releases my hand. I get in and he closes the door behind me.

'Sarina, the Pig and Whistle restaurant in the city, please.' The car pulls away and I see Shadow stepping back into the elevator.

It takes about half an hour to get through traffic into the city and Sarina stops the car out the front of the restaurant. There isn't any valet parking here so she will need to move on once I'm out of the car. I get out and head in. The usher sees me coming and heads over to me. Deano is sitting at the back of the restaurant. He waves at me and I point towards him as the usher arrives. He nods and escorts me over, pulling my chair for me to take a seat before disappearing again.

'Deano.'

He smiles. 'Hello, Foresight. So, you want me and my crew to join your team?'

Okay, so we are getting straight to it today, no niceties, straight to business. 'Yes, that is correct. I do.'

He looks at me for a moment, unfolding his napkin and laying it out across his lap. He always seems as cool as a cucumber. Like nothing ever fazes him. 'I know your team is connected to the government, but you are a black ops team with – how should I put it – full autonomy. Is that a fair statement?'

I nod. 'Yes, that about sums it up.'

He looks out over our surroundings for a few moments, just letting the world pass him by. 'You hunt the worst of the world, taking them out mostly in the cyber world but occasionally need some additional support. My team's kind of support. To finish the job or maybe to protect your team? That's what you want from us?'

'Yes, I want your team to be available to go where we need you, to get out hostages, rescue people, take bad people out or save our bacon if needed. You might get a bit more downtime than you are used to, but I will pay you well and provide you all with secure apartments as part of the deal. You'd be based at the same location where our team lives and works. Your team will be ready for when we need your expertise.'

He nods. 'The team and I aren't as young as we used to be. We have been talking about slowing down a little. This might be a good option for that. It's not just my choice though, the team will need to all agree.'

I nod. 'I would have expected nothing less.'

He nods. 'Good.' He picks up his drink and takes a sip, staring out into the distance.

'You seem troubled. Do you want to talk about it? Is it something I can help you with?' I ask.

He looks back at me, seemingly considering my statement. 'This life has its demons. My team and I have seen too many things, taken more lives for money than I can even comprehend. Most of them were bad people, but not all of them. I know we are mercenaries, that's what we do. We've always tried to be selective about who our clients are, align ourselves with the right kind of people, but we didn't always get it right. We have certainly been in some uncomfortable situations, some I wish we had not, but that is the way of things. My conscience is clear for the most part, but I feel the burden is weighing on my team. Maybe if we do some good, some real good for this world, it will help even the scales. I don't want to do it just for the money but because it's right.'

I understand the deep thought now. He's struggling with who his team are, who he is. It must be hard to decide how they as a team will finish up their tour of duty; will it be as they are? As guns for hire or will they choose to go down for a cause? They could use what skills they have nourished in blood to make a difference.

'I can see you have a lot to think about. I hope the decision is in my favour, but I will be here for you and your team no matter your decision. You all rose to the occasion when I was in need, helped me when no others could. You've all earned my respect and help, if you ever need it.'

We don't talk about the topic anymore. We eat, laugh and enjoy a few drinks. It's a good night. Deano really is a good man, no matter what he has done in his past. I can feel it. I just hope that I can help give him and his team a home, a family, in Vulcan.

Deano walks me to my car and as it approaches, he stops. 'Why is it that none of your cars have any drivers? Are they all controlled by people from your base or is there something more to this?' I can see he is very curious, unsure how we are making this happen. Should I introduce him to Sarina? I feel I can trust him.

Sarina must be thinking the same thing as I suddenly hear her over my earpiece. 'I think we can trust him. It's time you introduced Deano and me.'

I look at Deano. 'Would you like to find out?'

He looks at the vehicle and then back at me for a moment. He nods. 'Yes, I want to know.'

I smile. 'Then get in, I have someone to introduce you to.'

He looks a little confused but walks around to get in the other side. He pulls his door closed, looking around the car. I think he is assessing his risk. It would probably be second nature. I do the same since the day I first met his team.

'Deano, I would like you to meet Sarina. Sarina, meet Deano.'

He looks at me with a very puzzled look on his face. Until Sarina speaks.

'Hello, Deano. It is good to finally talk to you directly.' The car starts to pull away and he watches the steering wheel move around on its own. Sarina's avatar comes up on the car's main display panel and his eyes widen. I watch him. He is not sure what is going on but I start to see a realisation come across his face.

'Hello, Sarina. Are you AI? Is that how I would describe you?' He turns to look at me, expecting me to say something but I don't. I allow Sarina to answer.

'Yes, I suppose you could call me AI. I do prefer my given name from my creators though. Sarina is much nicer, don't you think?'

He looks at me again. 'How capable is she?'

I smile. 'Sarina is as capable of thought as either of us. Probably more, in some ways. She is still learning, but aren't we all? She was who was controlling your air and ground support during your rescue mission recently. She's growing stronger every day.'

Deano just looks at her avatar with a sort of amazement. 'Well, I guess it's great she is on our side.'

'Sarina is strictly need to know only, is that understood?'

He nods. 'Yes, understood. This is not a secret we would want to get out there or my team would have a tough job protecting her from the people who would want to claim her for their own gains.'

Sarina smiles. 'I guess that means you are joining our team then, Deano?'

He laughs. 'You caught that. Yes, I guess it does, if the rest of the team agrees. Give me a few days to discuss it with them and we'll be in touch.'

'Agreed. I will await your answer.' Sarina pulls up next to a black car. 'Your transport, Deano.'

He nods. 'Thanks. Wait, how did you know that was my car? No, don't worry, I don't want to know. Thanks for an interesting evening, Foresight.'

I smile. 'You too, Deano. It was a pleasure as always.'

CHAPTER 34

TUGGING AT THE LOOSE THREAD

I get back to my apartment, satisfied by how the meeting with Deano went. I am confident that his team will join the Vulcan fold, become part of our family. I walk in, putting my things on the kitchen bench, and walk out onto the balcony. It's a beautiful, clear night. I stand there looking out for a few minutes, just enjoying the peacefulness. I need to enjoy these moments when I can. there is a lot of work for us to do. It's good to just be though, feel for a moment.

'Foresight, I found something you need to see.'

Well, the serenity is over, for now at least. Back to the real world. I head back down to the lair. I walk through to the workspace and up to the main screen.

'Show me what you have.' I see chat history from WhatsApp. It has a generic name on the account, but it is threatening to release obscene photos of someone's daughter.

One line jumps out at me: *You know what we did to her? Do you want that plastered all over the internet? Do you want us to ruin her life even more? Get us the information we want, and we will keep these for personal use.*

I know why he did what he did. Why he leaked the information about the prime minister's travel route. Sick bastards did things to his daughter. He was just trying to protect her. I'd probably have done the same thing if I'd been in his shoes. 'Sarina, can you link these accounts to the terrorists and the deputy?'

'The deputy, yes. This is a screengrab off his mobile phone. The other account I am not one hundred per cent certain on. There is no real way I can verify if it was one of the people we took down. Unless I can get hold of the forensic images that were taken after they were all captured. I will see what I can get. I will also monitor the account and see where it leads me.'

'What else do we have? We need to find these photos, everything they have on that poor girl. I'm going to get an audience with the deputy. It's time we have a frank conversation. Can you get me his direct number?'

A few seconds go by and I see a message comes through to my phone. 'That is his personal number,' Sarina confirms. 'Not many have it, so I don't know if he will answer or not without recognising the number first, but I can try to put you through to him if you like?'

'Yes, please do.'

I read through my notes, making sure I have all of the details.

'I have him on the line for you now.'

I tap my earpiece and prepare myself for the conversation I am about to have. This could go one of two ways: he will admit what he has done or get angry and defensive. I guess we'll find out soon enough.

'Sir, my name is Foresight. I lead the Vulcan unit. We need to talk. I will assume you already know about what.'

The line is silent for a moment then I hear him clear his throat slightly. 'Yes, I believe I know why, but how about you tell me why?'

So he wants to make sure he is truly caught before he lets the cat out of the bag. I shouldn't be surprised – he is a politician.

'I know about what happened to your daughter and what you have been doing for the terrorist group to try to protect her. I need to know how far this all goes. Does this end with the groups' capture or is there some sort of puppet master I need to worry about?'

I can hear him start to cry. He is literally crying. I am on the phone with the deputy prime minister of Australia and he is a blubbering mess on the other end. 'I had to protect her; I had no choice. All I did was give them the travel route, nothing else, I swear. I didn't know what they would do. I figured our security teams would protect him. Now all of those people are dead and it's my fault.'

He's right, they are dead, the prime minister's whole detail because he gave them the information, but I don't blame him at all. Of course a father would try to protect his daughter. That's why they did what they did, they knew it would work.

'I will take my punishment for this, but I need to keep my daughter out of it. She has already been through enough. This would be the end for her – I can't let that happen.'

'I honestly don't know if I can do that, but I will try to keep her shielded. You have my word on that.'

I feel sorry for him a little – it's a tough position he was in. It will not be my decision what happens to him, that will land in the General's lap. I am happy about that, if I am honest. 'I will need everything you have. Emails, phone numbers, anything you have. Oh, and don't take any trips out of town.'

CHAPTER 35

THE GENERAL

I've been reviewing all of the evidence sent through with Sarina. It seems to correlate with the deputy PM's story; he was just a very powerful pawn in this game. With the forensics images, Sarina is able to obtain off the terrorist's phones, we found the person on the other end of the WhatsApp chat and a cloud storage account that housed several videos and pictures of the deputy's daughter. As we looked through the collection, I was horrified at the number of others who had content stored on them. At a glance, I count more than fifty other girls who have had horrible things done to them and it's all recorded for the manipulation or control of very important people.

'Sarina, we need to find out the identities of everyone featured in these files. Please put together a full list. Every one of these people has someone in their lives who could be a threat to national security. Who knows what they could be asking these people to do. We need to know who they are and find out what it is they have done or will do.'

I get up from my seat and start to pace 'I also want you to take control of this account, take the files and encrypt them so that no one apart from you will ever be able to decrypt the files. Once that is done, make sure these will never be seen by anyone else outside of our team ever again, scrub them from existence. I think the girls have already been through enough.'

It takes a few hours for Sarina and me to put together the list and generate a report for the General. 'I think it's time I take this up the chain a little to let him know what we are doing. Can you send through the report and get the General on the line for me? Make sure it's a secure connection.'

It takes a few minutes then Sarina is patching him through.

'Foresight, what do you have for me?'

I get up from my chair again and start to walk around the office. It helps me think. 'We have a problem, one that is going to get a little messy. When we brought down the terrorist group and rescued the prime minister, I had a nagging suspicion that something wasn't right. There was more to it than we knew. So, with the PM's knowledge, I dug deeper to find a potential mole in his camp. The problem is, I found one.'

'You found a mole in the PM's team?'

How do I say this? Just spit it out, I guess. 'The person who shared the PM's travel route was the deputy PM. He was being forced to do it via the main terrorist group member who orchestrated the attack on the PM. They had done some horrible things to his daughter and threatened to share photos and videos of the ordeal. He couldn't allow that, so he did what they asked. He didn't think it would get anyone killed but it did.'

'That's a serious accusation, Foresight. Do you have evidence?'

I pause. 'Yes, we have evidence, and he has confessed to me. It has been included as part of evidence. That's not the end of it though.'

I hear a noise on the other end of the line, someone has entered the room. I wait for him to dismiss whoever it was. 'Sorry, what do you mean that's not the end of it? How much worse could it get than having the deputy PM involved?'

'When we traced the evidence trail back, we found something, something very concerning. A cloud storage area that had more than fifty folders, all of them for different girls who had been put through the same atrocities. These are daughters of very powerful people.' I look down the list. 'One of them is your daughter. What are you doing for them, General?'

The line is quiet for a moment. 'Is this line secure?'

I look over at Sarina's avatar and she nods. 'Yes, it is secure.'

I wait for the General to explain what the hell is going on. 'I haven't done anything for them yet. They told me when the time is right, they will call on me to do something for them. I was not to question it, just do whatever it is they ask. It's my daughter. I would do anything for her, but I have not had to yet. I was hoping I could find them first, find out who it was. I haven't been able to do that yet, but it looks like you might have. Did you get the only copies of the files?'

'Yes, I think I have all copies of the files. The only remaining copies are encrypted so well, I don't even know if I could break them.' I hear a sigh of relief, it would be a weight off his shoulders knowing those files are gone. 'It's not over though. This doesn't stop with the terrorist group, someone else is pulling the strings. I don't know who.' I need to flush them out, make them come at us somehow.

The General must be thinking the same thing. 'Now that you have the files, how about we shake the tree a little and see who falls out? What do you say, Foresight, are you up for a game? It will need to be a closed group op, just your team and me. I will push back, let them come at me and your team can flush them out, do what I know Vulcan does best. Is the rest of your team looped in on this?'

'No, this is a closed loop at the moment, but I will read them in, then we can shake the hornet's nest. Actually, if we are going to do anything like we would normally do, it's probably going to be more like kicking the nest and then setting it alight. That seems to be more how we roll around here.'

The General laughs. 'You are right. For a black ops team, you really don't do subtlety very well. You are the best, but you could learn to lay low a little, I think, do things a little quieter at times. I guess that wouldn't be Vulcan though, would it, not your style.' He laughs again then suddenly goes quiet for a moment. 'Thank you for taking care of those files, protecting the girls. You truly are meant to do this job.'

I don't say anything back to that – there is no need. 'What is the plan, General? What are you going to do?' He needs to do something to provoke them, to force their hand to react, maybe even lash out at him.

'I am going to tell them I am going to report what I have to the agency, get my team to hunt them down. Tell them I will make them pay for what they did and there isn't anything they can do to stop me, they need to watch their backs. I think that should provoke them to lash out at me, show me who's boss.'

Yes, that could work. Maybe too well. Talk about kicking the hornet's nest.

He continues. 'I will get one of my back molars fitted with a tracker, one I can activate by biting down hard. It will mean if they snatch me, I will pass the tracking tests. When I am alone and ready for your team to do its thing, you will see me activate the tracker.'

'So, essentially, you plan to piss them off, draw them out to either snatch you, potentially try and kill you or threaten you. Are you sure you want to use yourself as bait? I am sure my team can track them down with a bit of time.'

He's quiet for a few moments and when he speaks again there's a coldness in his voice that makes goosebumps rise on my forearms. 'No. This needs to be how it is. We can't wait for them to do something else to any children or force someone to do something horrendous for their gain. It needs to stop and now is the best time. They'll be on the back foot after you took out the terrorist group, probably unsure how they should proceed. We need to force a move before they can regroup properly.'

I agree. It is the best plan we have and we can't sit by and wait for them to do something to someone else. 'Okay, send me the tracking details. We will go dark but we will be watching and waiting. Be safe.'

I hope this goes to plan.

'Bring your A-game, Foresight. I think I am going to need it. Get your strike team ready, this could get a little bumpy.'

The line goes dead. He is gone. I have a bad feeling about all of this. We don't have any control of the situation. We are leaving it all to chance but I don't have much of a choice – we need to bring them out into the open.

'Sarina, call the team in, it's time to prepare. I have another call to make.'

I search through my contacts for Deano. I need to force his decision, I am going to need his team for this. I hit the call button. It rings for a few moments.

'Foresight, who has your team provoked today?'

I laugh. He already has us pegged well, he knows why I have called.

'No one yet, Deano, but I have a feeling the day is only young. Have you made a decision?'

The line is dead quiet for a moment. 'Yes, we have made a decision. We are in.'

I relax a little with that answer. I don't know what I would have done if they had declined my offer. It would be hard to put the same level of faith in any other team.

'That's great to hear. Sarina will send you all the details of your new homes. Activate your team, they will be needed soon.'

'Yes, ma'am. Consider it done.'

I turn and see Shadow, Hammer and Glimmer walk through the door. A few moments later DeadlyRose arrives as well. 'Team, we have some more work to do. The op is not over. We found some loose ends and I pulled at them. We have found ourselves a completely new rabbit hole to go down. It involves the General, my direct commander, offering himself up as bait to help catch the puppet masters who have been controlling all of this from a distance. I will need your best work on this, no mistakes.

'Deano's strike team will be joining us in the coming hours. They have agreed to join Vulcan. They will be part of our family, here to support our missions and protect us if necessary.'

They all nod. I can see a smile on Shadows face, he is very happy about that.

'Sarina will share what we have and give you all a rundown on what the plan is. We will be going dark, waiting for the snake to show its head. When it does we need to be prepared to strike physically and virtually. It needs to be swift and precise.'

They all quickly move to their stations.

'Vulcan, it's time to hunt.'

CHAPTER 36

GOING DARK

They snatched the General a few days ago. Took him from his car when he stopped at an intersection. The usual suspect black van stopped in front of him, guns out, pulled him from the car. Phone, wallet, and clothes were all thrown from the van. They must have stripped him naked to ensure he didn't have any trackers. We tried to track their movements, but they slipped us. They knew how to keep out of sight.

If I am honest, I'm a little worried about what they have done to him. The longer it takes us to find him or for him to activate the tracker the more I feel he won't make it out alive. I knew it was a bad idea. The General is a soldier though. He is not just an officer but an experienced soldier. I have to keep faith that he can look after himself. He will signal us somehow or our team will find him. Everyone makes mistakes. They will make a mistake and we will be watching for it.

I have spent a few hours this morning cracking all the General's accounts, emails, messaging, anything that might point us to who the target might be, who took him. I have been trawling through everything, like I used to before Sarina, before Vulcan. It's good to get back to basics, to do what I do best.

I don't find anything of interest, so I pass it over to Sarina to have a second look over it all. She might find something I've missed. I look around at the team. They have been working hard the last few days. It looks like they all need some sleep, not that any of them would volunteer to leave their post.

'I think you should all get some downtime, go get some sleep and come back with some fresh eyes. If I find anything I will let you know.'

They slowly all get up and leave, even Shadow. He hasn't taken a break in over thirty hours.

I go grab a coffee and sit back down in my chair. Come on, General, help us out. Show us a clue. Maybe we missed something on the terrorists' phones, maybe there is a communication to someone outside of the group. We weren't looking for that at the time. I load up the images in Cellabrite and start to search through the phone's contents, messages, emails, photos. I look at the metadata on some of the images, not of the girls, but just other things they took photos of, streets, buildings. Maybe when they were staking out the area.

'Sarina, can you correlate all the metadata from all of the photos from the terrorist group that we have? Does it give us any GPS locations that are frequented?' The photos with the girls have had the data removed, but many of the other images on the phones have not. Sarina starts to put them all up on a map on the screen wall. They are spread all over the country, but there does seem to be one location that is starting to get a few more hits. Adelaide, on the north side. I wonder what is there. The markers are spread over a few kilometres.

'Sarina, focus everything we have on this area. If they are here, we need to find them. Look for anything suspicious in traffic cameras, satellites. Find something we can focus on.'

I take a drink of my coffee and watch the images fly across the screens. Sarina is fast-forwarding multiple videos and zooming and un zooming satellite images. It's a little chaotic. Suddenly, I see it, a quick view of someone being pulled out of the car, with some sort of cover over their head.

'Sarina, stop, go back slightly. Someone was just taken from a car with a cover over their head. It could be him, it could be the General.'

She goes back, taking a closer look over the footage that just passed and then stops on a slightly blurry image. It could be someone as I suspect or it could be a bag or something. She focuses on cleaning up the image. It takes a few moments and then as clear as day you can see a man in boxer shorts and a black bag over his head with what looks like like zip ties binding his wrist.

'Find that facility, Sarina. Find who we are up against. Also, tell the team we have found something. No need to rush back to the lair just yet, but we are making progress.'

I dig into the details on the property. It's registered to an offshore entity, one that looks familiar. Then it dawns on me. It's a government facility, used by ASIO and ASD to do unsavoury questioning. Who the hell is pulling the strings? We need to be careful. Why would ASIO be involved in this? Do we have some sort of rogue, splinter cell? We need to be very careful, go dark until we know what is happening and if that is the General or just some poor bastard who is being interrogated by spooks.

'Sarina, put us in lockdown. No one in or out until further notice. I think we are just about to walk into a turf war between government agencies, and I don't want to leave us unawares. That's probably who was following us the other night.'

CHAPTER 37

LOCKDOWN

Life in lockdown is pretty normal. We don't usually go out much anyway. We're just a little more alert than usual and all of the security controls for the building are on. Sarina is monitoring all activity around the building for anything that could pre-empt some sort of attack on our facility. Shadow and I have been focusing on the location that could be holding the General. I told the rest of the team to get some downtime. Once we can validate where they are holding him, it will be all hands on deck. We've been trying for hours to find a way into the facility, to get access to video or audio. We're thinking we're going to need to find a new way through their security.

I know they would have feeds in and out of the facilities. These are often used as cold sites, a location they can work and plan atrocities. Nothing that they would ever admit to the general public or the politicians running the country because they don't really run the country, these agencies do. They pull the strings, they steer the ship in the direction they want.

I find a way to use the logj4 vulnerability to manipulate one of their security platforms to give me full command and control functionality. It's one of those rare vulnerabilities that is a 10/10 on the CVE scale. This one is nice and new. I have been watching security teams scramble to lock this down for weeks. I bet they haven't gotten out to the cold sites yet.

I run the script with the modified command to allow me to exploit the java logging function. I have a console, I got you now. I configure a secure connection to the network and anonymise my activity; I don't want them to find me just yet.

'Shadow, we are in. Can you give me a hand getting into the surveillance system? You seem to have a knack for breaking their security protections.'

He slides over to take a look at the information then slides back over to his desk. His fingers glide over the keyboard. It's almost like watching a pianist play, it's almost magical. He is in. We have full control.

'Sarina, put the feed up on our screens. Let's find the General, if he is in there.' About eighty camera feeds jump up on the screen. We all look, trying to find him. They have a few people in here but there, there he is. 'That one, Sarina, that one.'

She expands the screen. That is definitely him. He looks a little worse for wear, but he is alive. Sarina moves the camera to get a better view. The General notices it. He looks at the camera for a moment and then nods. He must know it's us because he straightens his shoulders a little, his resolve solidified once more.

'Sarina, tell Deano it's time for his team to get ready. We will need to get them down to Adelaide ready to make a move. Reach out to Boeing again. We need to borrow a big bird, one that can carry our convoy and personnel. Tell them we need it yesterday.'

About ten minutes pass. 'The plane will be ready for the team in thirty minutes. The team is loading the convoy with their equipment and heading out.'

I nod. 'Tell them Shadow and I will be coming with them. We will take the command centre vehicle. Make sure you have full functionality, Sarina, we are going to need your help, I am sure of it. We are going to need a lot more than brute strength to get into that place; we are going to need to be a little creative. The rest of you, once the action starts, we need you to distract them as best you can, help us get an advantage. If they retaliate, push them back and go dark if you need to. It's time to go pick a fight.'

CHAPTER 38

HEADING OUT TO BAT

We have arrived at Boeing's airfield. We brought three of the armoured vehicles and the tricked-out command centre vehicle. It is literally a moving data centre with enough computing power to do anything we need with multiple 5G and satellite connections. If we weren't used to having Sarina's quantum computing power at our fingertips, this setup would indeed be pretty impressive, but alas, it is still hard to go from a Ferrari to a Hyundai. It's just how it is.

As we approach the plane, the rear door is dropped and we drive on in. We don't get out and no one asks questions. As soon as we are stationary, the flight team secures our vehicles and raises the door. Once it is all in place, I hear the engines turn over and we quickly launch down the runway and into the air. It's a short flight to Adelaide, around an hour before we start to descend. When we touch down on the tarmac, the flight crew disconnect our vehicles and as soon as we stop, they lower the back door signalling for us to exit. 'Let's go, Sarina, we are clear to move. Make sure you thank the team for us and tell them we will see them soon.'

We make our way quickly to the site, keeping a slight distance to ensure they don't know what is about to happen. 'Team, we need to know what sort of security systems they have ingrained in that site. Any ideas on how we can get past it would be great. We already have the cameras so you can keep us off the feeds but every door and window is secured and there is going to be isolation zones, lockdown protocols, this will be the hardest site to get in and out of that any of us have ever been involved with. If we get this wrong, the General could be killed and the rest of us could spend a very long time in some federal black hole for espionage or whatever trumped-up charge they make up to hold us.'

Shadow and I go over the blueprints of the site, comparing everything with the video feeds. This is not going to be easy. We're going to need to find a way of taking control of the door lock systems. These are on an internal OT network, isolated from the camera network. The only way we are getting access to this is to get inside somehow. We need to either get an access card and pin or find another way in.

Wait, hang on. We are an ASD black ops team. We don't need to break in, we can just walk in as we see fit. Once we are inside, we can breach the OT network getting us through to the other area currently in use.

'Sarina, reach out to ASD command. We need to use the black ops site, for let's say, a base of operations for a strike on a potential target in the area. It's the truth. They just don't know how close that target is.' I hope this is the right move. 'Team, if we do this, they will know we are coming, and the benefit of surprise will be gone. It could get real messy real fast. Are we all good with the plan?'

There is silence for a moment before Deano responds. 'We are with you, Foresight. Let's make some noise.'

Shadow nods. Okay, we are a go then.

'Foresight, you now have the authorisation to use the site. They indicated that an ASIO team is currently using the western side of the facility and we have been approved for eastern side access. The western part of the facility is off-limits due to the sensitivity of the operation under way.'

Sensitivity of the operation, hey? I would think so, taking a General who runs the ASD hostage in broad daylight and keeping him captive with a few other prisoners is certainly going to raise eyebrows if that gets out. We need to find out who in ASIO is pulling these strings, who the puppet master is before we get blindsided. We need to make the first move, remove their power.

We approach the gates of the facility heading to the eastern side access. Sarina sends through access codes we have been given and the gates open. We drive through to the roller doors on that side of the facility, and they open as we approach. We pull into the facility, forming a defensive formation with the vehicles. We hold our position, watching our surroundings. 'Sarina, are we clear to exit the vehicles?'

'You are clear to proceed. There are no other people in this part of the facility. We are alone, and you are ready to move to stage two.'

I grab my gear, ensuring my vest and weapon. I check the clips and load the first round into the chamber, taking the safety off before placing it in my holster. I also double-check Shadow's vest. I don't think I could deal with it if something happened to him. 'Deano, let's move. Defensive positions but keep it low key in case anyone is watching. We don't want them to be too suspicious just yet.'

We make our way through the facility until we get to an office area near the edge of our approved eastern zone. I get out my laptop and connect it into the network behind one of the access panels. It is not restricted by mac address or anything so I pretty much have free run of the network. I look for the control servers. Got them. I take a breath and focus. It's game time.

I get to work manipulating, adjusting my approach until I find a way in, some default credentials left in a control server, now I have some admin rights. I add in access for our team and give Sarina a backdoor into the platform, a bridge between the OT and physical network. I clean my tracks and then look up at the team. 'Are you all ready? Sarina, get ready to move the vehicles. We might need to get out of here very fast. Can you confirm if the General is still in the same location?' I watch as the team checks their weapons, prepares for what awaits us on the other side of that door.

'The location is confirmed but you might want to hurry. There is currently a man standing in front of him holding a gun up to his head.'

Oh shit, we need to move.

'Deano, it's time for you to do what you do best. Clear the way and we will carry him out.' He nods, signalling his men. They open the door, sweeping through each room as they advance, one by one taking out any targets in their path. It's fast and silent, barely a sound. Shadow and I follow along behind slowly, I have my weapon drawn but it is unlikely I will need it.

Deano signals his men to halt. We must be nearing the location. He signals again. I am not sure what they are about to do but we prepare ourselves, crouching down near a wall ready for what is about to come next. Then they move – gunfire, smoke, it's chaos. Were we quick enough? Did we get to the General in time?

I peer through the smoke; there is a body on the ground with someone standing over them. I walk a little closer and see it's Deano standing over them. Whoever is on the ground is dead, a pool of blood forming on the floor beneath the body.

My heart starts to sink. We didn't make it. He is gone. I kneel next to the body and turn them over. It's not him, it is not the General.

'Where is he?' I ask, looking around.

Deano and his men continue to move through the facility, searching each room one by one, with no sign of him or anyone else.

'Foresight, there is a group exiting the building on the roof. Two helicopters are inbound very fast. I have already dispatched two of the Loyal Wingmen drones when the fighting started but they won't be here for at least fifteen more minutes. I don't know how we are going to stop them.'

'Sarina, bring the vehicles around to pick us up. We need to find a way to stop them. Shadow, you ever hacked a chopper before?'

He looks at me like I am crazy. I probably am, but there has to be a way to stop them. Interfere with the signalling, radar, controls, there has to be something. 'Sarina, if they get on that helicopter don't lose them, we need to know where they are going. Can we commandeer any air support, anything in the area? We need options or they are going to get away.'

We head to the garage entrance and our vehicles roll in. We all climb in getting ready to move. As we approach the door, I see one of the helicopters hover down in front of the door. They have what looks to be a Gatling gun pointed right at us.

Oh shit. 'Get down!' I scream at my team.

They open fire and the noise of bullets hitting the vehicle is deafening, like a jackhammer pounding against the sides. This is not good, we need to get out of here fast.

'Sarina, how far away is the air support?' They will be loading the General in the other helicopter as we speak, we need to move. BOOOM! The helicopter explodes in a ball of fire, pieces flying everywhere, shaking our vehicles. My ears are ringing slightly. Sarina activated the weapons systems on the vehicles and blew them out of the sky. I bet they didn't expect that. The front vehicle rams the remains of the helicopter, pushing it back out of the way, clearing the path for the rest of us. It falls in behind the last vehicle and we circle back around the building.

But the other helicopter is already in the air and it's pulling away very quickly. They are getting away and there is nothing I can do about it.

CHAPTER 39

FAILURE IS NOT AN OPTION

I pace back and forth just outside the vehicle. Our failure may have just cost the General his life. I won't except that as the outcome. This is not over yet. I punch the side of the vehicle in frustration, instantly regretting it when my knuckles sting with sharp pain.

'Foresight, are you okay?' Shadow is watching me.

'Does it look like I am okay? We screwed up Shadow, we really screwed up.' He moves closer reaching out towards me, but I dismiss it, brushing off his touch. 'What do we have? There needs to be a next move,' I snap.

He looks at me for a moment and decides to just let it go. I feel a prickle of guilt for doing it but I don't need to be coddled, I need answers. I can see he doesn't like me shutting him out but I need to focus on the mission.

Sarina answers my question. 'We found the helicopter, but the General is gone. I am trying to track the movements from there, but it looks like they have made a clean get away.'

I scrunch my fists, trying to control my anger. I need to keep a clear head.

Shadow watches me patiently, letting me have my space. I stop, taking a deep breath clearing my mind. *What is the plan, Sam? What is the plan? Think, Sam, think.*

'Sarina, continue your search, we need to find them.' I turn to look at Deano and his team who have set up a perimeter. 'Deano, ready your team to move. We can't stay here.' He nods and gives the order to leave to his team.

We all get into the vehicles and leave the site. I will have some explaining to do later about what happened here but that will need to wait. Shadow gently takes my hand, looking at the damage I caused when I thought it was a good idea to punch an armoured vehicle. Not the smartest idea I've had.

'Are you okay?'

I nod. It hurt, but nothing is broken. He doesn't press for anything further.

Two more hours pass with nothing, not a sign. This is not the way I pictured all of this going. Failure is not something I am used to. General, where the hell are you? Time to regroup. 'Shadow, do you have any bunkers nearby? We need somewhere to lay low until we figure this out.' With what just went down here we are going to have some heat on us; they will be hunting for us as well. We need to find the General and plan the next move. If we get it wrong again it is certain he will pay of it with his life, if he hasn't already.

He nods. 'Yes, I do indeed. Sarina, activate the nearby bunker, get it ready for our arrival.'

'Vulcan, I know you are tired and probably as frustrated as I am, but we need our best work now. We need to be an unstoppable force. Let's pick ourselves up and dust ourselves off. Time to finish this on our terms.'

ALSO BY CRAIG FORD

FORESIGHT

HAVE YOU EVER DREAMED OF BEING A HACKER?

To anyone who meets her, Samantha is just a good-hearted teenager who wants to finish school and go to college.

Yet she has a secret life...

She has spent years living two lives, one as Sam, which the world sees most, and one as Foresight, who Sam feels is her true self, where she is a passionate and gifted hacker.

She has never found a system she could not bend to her will.

She is the essence of a true magician within the dark recesses of the web, which many dare not enter.

Foresight and Sam never mix.

This is something that Sam goes to extreme lengths to ensure.

These two very different lives however may be veering towards an unstoppable collision course.

The weave of tension and intrigue grows beyond her comprehension as she dives beneath the deep dark corners of the hacker world to really discover what she is made of.

SHADOW

HAVE YOU EVER DREAMED OF BEING A HACKER?

In this thrilling second instalment to the *Foresight* series, *Shadow* offers a fresh insight into the opposing hacker of the series – Shadow.

Shadow must make choices that will lead him down many paths that were never expected in the outset.

Find out what makes Shadow tick and experience the thrilling events from *Foresight* from a completely new perspective.

Shadow is fun, dangerous and dives further into the hacking world that *Foresight* first exposed.

Will the possibilities of the digital world help Shadow find his place in reality also...?

"A devilishly clever second book of the series that weaves more depth to the plot and characters. Exceptional..." Maxwell, Indie Book reviewer

THE SHADOW WORLD

BE WARY OF THE SHADOW WORLD AROUND US AND KNOW THIS BOOK IS YOUR DEFENCE AGAINST THE DARKNESS.

Much like in your house, shadows can be scary until you turn the light on. The same goes for the online world. Sometimes when we do not know what we are looking at or dealing with, it can be overwhelming and potentially dangerous.

We are here to help you navigate your way around this online world, arming you with your very own knowledge torch.

Together we can light up these shadowy areas of the online world to know what you may soon experience, what to believe online and what to be cautious of. There are times when you may mess up, but we are here to tell you that you are not alone. We can show you how to get out of those shadows and back into the safety of the light.

This book is the creation of experts who share their experience and knowledge with you, so your world is less at risk of slipping into the Shadow World beyond your device screens…

Plus, you may find a new interest in the cybersecurity world along the way!

CYBER UNICORNS
www.cyberunicorns.com.au